Confessions:

Secrets & Lies

Revealed

BROWN GIRLS BOOKS

Houston, Texas * Washington, D.C.

Confessions: Secrets & Lies Revealed © 2020

Brown Girls Books, LLC

www.BrownGirlsBooks.com

ISBN: 978-1-944359-83-6 (Digital)

978-1-944359-84-3 (Print)

TABLE OF CONTENTS

LETTER FROM THE PUBLISHERS

Dear Reader,

Brown Girls Books is excited to bring you *Confessions: Secrets & Lies Revealed,* a collection of short stories that delve into the topic of what happens when the things we try to keep from those we love, come bursting out.

Thank you for your support of this amazing group of writers. We are so ecstatic to bring you stories from established authors and even more excited to introduce you to a bevy of new writers. It's always a difficult task to narrow our selections down from the mounds of submissions, but we're proud of the final 15. And for the first time, thrilled to have two men in our ranks!

Brown Girls Books was established to not only give voice to fan favorites, but to give publishing opportunities to talented writers who might not have otherwise had them. Not because they weren't deserving, but because of changes within the publishing industry.

Know that we greatly value and appreciate your support. We work very hard to bring you quality reading material that not only satisfies your hunger for a good story, but that also gives talented writers the opportunity to tell their stories and have their voices heard. That is at the very heart of Brown Girls Book's existence.

What you don't see is that behind the scenes, the contributors have created a strong friendship, and supportive bond that encourages and motivates each other through their professional aspirations. They have also created an accountability system, where they support each other and propel each other toward greatness. We hope you enjoy *Confessions* and we appreciate your support.

Peace, love and literature,
Victoria and ReShonda

1

IDLE HANDS

By Nicole Bird-Faulkner

I stepped out of LaGuardia Airport and was met by the most disrespectful chill that I've ever felt. My visits home to New York were mainly in the spring and summer for this very reason.

I turned up the collar on my thin leather jacket. While sufficient for Atlanta winters, it was a joke to the professional winters of New York. I dug in my bag for my hat and tugged it as low as possible over my ears. I pulled my long locs out of the ponytail holder and made a makeshift scarf out of my hair.

Just as I was doing this, a black Range Rover pulled up and the window slid down. Though it had been years since I'd seen him, I immediately knew the man behind the wheel was Aiden.

"Shorty, you need a ride? You look a little cold." Aiden's smile lit up his entire face.

He didn't wait for me to answer as he parked the truck, jumped out, grabbed my bag and threw it in the back seat. Though we had talked almost every day for the past three weeks, seeing him in person made me feel like I was cheating on Bryce, and I blamed my sister, Regina.

The night I rejected Bryce's proposal, my sister and my best friend, Layla, decided to reveal to me that they both thought I had commitment phobia. That night, Regina deemed herself "the fixer" and the "finder of bootleg boyfriends." Two bottles of wine and a phony Facebook account later, Regina, aka *Jacqueline*, found my top three exes, and apparently, these three held the key to why I rejected Bryce's proposal, along with a three-carat diamond ring.

Bryce and I had been together for three years. I thought I was in love but I knew I never wanted to get married. He knew this, too. After I said no, he said he needed space, booked a flight for L.A. so he could think, and I hadn't heard from him since.

Regina found Aiden's Facebook page covered with a slew of half-naked ladies on flyers for parties he was hosting. He had become *AK-47*, one of New York's top producers, but to me he was still Aiden Kage from high school. Within minutes of finding his profile, Regina had all of his contact information and had already sent a direct message on my behalf. I couldn't stand her sometimes.

As for Bryce, he was still M.I.A. My mother used to say, "Idle hands are the devil's workshop." So here I was, only three weeks later, flying to New York for Thanksgiving to hang out with Aiden Kage for a couple of days before going to my mother's house for the actual holiday.

She would kill me if she knew I was here, especially since my mother and Aiden's mother still spoke and this is something they would want to talk about.

Aiden snapped me from my thoughts by placing his hands on my hips.

"You're so damn beautiful, Michaela," he said before leaning in for a kiss.

My first instinct was to push him away but his lips felt like home.

"All right, lovebirds. Move it." An NYPD officer interrupted our greeting with a smirk on his face.

After I slid inside, Aiden walked over to the driver's side of the car, jumped in and leaned in for another quick peck. He adjusted the heat on my side and turned the radio on to '90s R&B.

"Thank you. I'm seriously not made for this weather anymore."

"What do you expect when you come up here in a jacket?" he said flicking my collar with his finger.

"This is all I need in Atlanta," I said, sinking into the warmth of the seat.

"So, we have two days together. What do you want to do? I cleared my entire calendar for you. We can go wherever you want or we can just stay indoors. We have a lot of catching up to do," he said with a wink.

Regina warned me that the *first* always had a quick release button on your panties. This familiarity between us made Regina's warning all the more prophetic.

"Maybe we should stay outdoors as much as possible, Aiden," I said. "We haven't seen each other in a while and maybe it'll be good to use these two days to talk."

He sat up straight. "You want to spend the next two days talking?" he asked, then let out a deep sigh. "Listen, I'm going to be honest with you." He reached for my hand and intertwined our fingers. "I don't want to be your friend. You are my first real love. So, if you're looking for a BFF, I can't do that."

"But we aren't the same people we were in high school, Aiden. I'm definitely not who I was then and you are AK-47, now," I said, teasing him. "I'm shocked no one has locked you down." I searched his face for a smile, but he just stared straight ahead not reacting to my slight jab. "I don't think I'll ever not love you," I continued. "I would just like to get to know you again."

"But there may be some things you don't like," Aiden said, removing his hand from mine.

"Like what?" My curiosity was piqued, but the only answer I received was his silence and the sound of Mint Condition's *"What Kind of Man Would I Be"* on the radio. Aiden turned it down, leaving us to sit in silence.

Twenty quiet minutes later, we were standing in front of Aiden's condo on the 18th floor in Long Island City. He unlocked the door and reached for my hand to lead me inside.

"Damn." I stood in the foyer, eyes wide, staring at the huge living room decorated with black leather couches and a television the size of a movie screen.

My reaction broke his silence. "You like it?" he asked, placing the keys on a small table by the door. I nodded as I walked inside looking around like I was in a museum. The condo was the epitome of a bachelor pad if all bachelor pads were mini mansions.

I took off my coat, laid it on the couch and walked over to the windows that encased a picturesque view of the Manhattan skyline.

"This is amazing, Aiden."

As I took in the view, I felt the warmth of his body behind me and his hands around my waist.

"I'm just glad you're here to see it."

I felt his chest on my back and his arms tighten around me. I gazed through the window and noticed our reflection in the glass. His thick, warm lips kissed my neck as if he remembered the very spot he had once discovered. I closed my eyes to take the feeling in. My body knew him and responded. He was an old habit and I was ready to relapse.

He turned me to face him. I felt a small protest queuing up in the back of my mind, but he kissed me deeply and quieted any little bit of fight that lingered. Regina was right. All I felt was a quick release.

*****

The next morning, I woke up in a room that was the size of my entire condo and with man I hadn't seen in a decade. I lifted my head from the pillow; his arm was wrapped around me as if he was scared I'd make a run for it while he slept. I sat up trying not to stir him and pulled the plush white comforter over my chest.

I looked over at Aiden. His body had become chiseled and strong. The lean, athletic teenager I once knew had become a full-grown man. But after last night, I realized we both did some growing up.

The last time we were together, we were young - studying the clock to make sure we had enough time to do what we weren't supposed to be doing. We were more focused on what was happening than who we were with. There was no intentionality, there was only excitability. There was only focus and a sneaky resolve. We didn't really enjoy each other, but now...there was experience behind his touch; an urgency to please. We met in that room with the history of new lovers and it made for the best sex I ever had.

I rose from the bed, wrapped in his comforter, and left him with a white sheet covering his body, revealing the contours of his frame. I stood in front of the floor to ceiling window and stared over the water to see snowflakes kissing the skyline. The city was beautiful in the winter.

"I could get used to that," Aiden said, leaning on his side watching me.

"Used to what?" I teased, looking over my shoulder.

"Seeing your beautiful body first thing in the morning. Come here."

I let the comforter fall off my shoulder and turned to him with playful seduction. "You mean this beautiful body?" I raised my eyebrows while teasing him with peeks of flesh.

"You better come over here or I'm going to come get you." He sat up in the bed and the sheet dropped to his lap. While I had no expectations of rekindling old flames, I was definitely enjoying the spark that was between us.

I walked over to the bed, still covered by the comforter, and stood in front of him. He placed his hands under the comforter, slowly caressed the back of my thighs, rested them on my behind and then traveled up to my waist. His hands were warm, soft and inviting. He unwrapped the comforter from my body and let it fall to the floor.

"Damn, Michaela."

I smirked and licked my lips, readying myself.

Aiden leaned back on the bed and rested on his elbows. His eyes studied every inch of my body. He pulled me on top of him and we only had a sliver of sheet between us. He placed his hands on the sides of my face and pulled me in for a deep, long kiss. A soft moan escaped from my lips and only seemed to incite Aiden more.

I moved my hand down to his chin and lifted it until his lips found mine again. He kissed me with a passion that we had never shared before. I sunk deep into his kisses but was interrupted by the lyrics of Notorious B.I.G.'S "Warning" coming from his phone:

Who the f@$% is this?
Paging me at 5:46 in the morning,
crack of dawn and now I'm yawning,
wipe the cold out my eye
See who's this paging me and why?

"Are we still doing ringtones?" I whispered, inches from his lips, trying to lighten the mood.

He chuckled and dropped his head onto the side of my neck. He kissed it and rose from the bed.

I rested on my side as he looked at me apologetically and answered the phone with a soft, "Hey." He gave me a quick wink as he walked to the bathroom not attempting to cover his nakedness.

His tone was relaxed and sweet, like he was familiar with whoever was on the other end. I heard him explaining his whereabouts in muffled tones. He said something about having to work and needing a minute to handle business in the City before "coming home." While I didn't expect him to say he was lying next to his ex in bed, I didn't expect him to blatantly lie about being with me. I wondered who could be on the other end of that call that deserved the explanation he gave and wasn't he already home?

I stood from the bed and grabbed his t-shirt from the floor. I couldn't find my underwear and realized they were somewhere in the living room. Our clothes were scattered throughout his condo and my suspicions were telling me to collect my belongings when Aiden opened the bathroom door.

"Hey, where are you going?" he asked, searching my face for answers.

My tone was quick and curt. "Sounded like you needed some privacy." I kept marching toward the living room hearing my bare feet slap on the hardwood floors.

Aiden grabbed his boxers off of the floor, put them on, nearly falling over, and followed me with a look of concern on his face.

"Michaela, what's up?" He grabbed my arm and turned me to face him. "We need to finish what we started, boo," he said, raising his eyebrows and licking his lips.

I looked back at him, realizing I hadn't even asked him if he was seeing anyone. Hell, he hadn't asked me and I didn't offer either. I didn't want to know because deep inside I knew that whatever was happening over these two days was more important to me than what was on the other side of that question. There was still someone in my life, even if we were on a break. And if there was someone else in his life, then we both rendered them insignificant, at least temporarily.

My countenance softened as he held my hand and walked me over to his couch.

"What do you want to know?"

"What do you want to tell me?" I retorted, with a little attitudinal residue.

He sighed and leaned back on the couch closing his eyes. "Look, I didn't expect to speak to you one day and have you here with me a few weeks later, Michaela." He opened his eyes and rested his hand on my thigh. "There is something about you that I still want. I still love you. You know that, right?"

I nodded, acknowledging what he said but was still waiting to draw his attention back to the relational elephant in the room.

"So, are you seeing someone?" I decided not to mince words. Direct questions usually got direct answers. Usually. I figured we would both have to do the big reveal, but I would let him go first.

"I mean," he said, scratching the top of his head, which had been his tell since high school.

"Looks like you haven't changed much," I said, hitting him with one of the throw pillows.

He grinned. "What about you?" he asked, leaving the question unanswered.

"What about me?" I asked. If he was going to dive into denial, I was going to backstroke in it. I had two options - acknowledge those who were ruminating in the background of our lives or act like they didn't exist. One would smack us both in the face bringing this throwback tryst to a screeching halt, the other would allow us to at least enjoy the hours we had ahead of us. I could do it for a day but after this, I would cut ties with Aiden and head back to reality. Both options sucked but at least one let me have a good time. Ignorance was bliss, even if it was trifling.

I rose from my seat and straddled Aiden's lap. "Aiden," I said, putting my arms around his neck. "We both have lives outside of these doors. We can return to them tomorrow or return to them now. I know I have some years to catch up on and I would like to do that."

"Our own little Vegas, huh?" he said, nuzzling my earlobe.

"What happens here, stays here," I said, shutting off my conscience. As I kissed the man who was the first to tell me he loved me, I knew that New York was not Vegas and what happened here was going to follow me home whether I liked it or not.

*****

Living out those missed hoe years, huh?

My thumbs moved fast across my phone screen as I answered Regina's text.

Don't be mad since you used all of yours up.

Her response was instant.

Hush, child. Are you going home or will you be giving thanks under Aiden tomorrow?

I smiled as I replied.

Actually, Aiden is driving me to Mommy's house now. But I did give thanks…a whole lot of thanks. Two whole days of thanks. Lol. I'll call you later.

She replied: *Just nasty.* ☺

Must be in the genes. LOL

I pressed send on my final text to Regina and placed my phone in my purse. Aiden reached for my hand and interlocked our fingers before pulling them to his lips for a kiss.

"I've really enjoyed you. How long are you staying in New York?" he asked.

"Until Sunday. Are you going to your mom's tomorrow?"

He shook his head. "She's coming over to my house in New Jersey. She's come to me for the past couple of years. She hates it though because I get Thanksgiving catered and she thinks I sold out." He let out a laugh revealing those adorable dimples that I knew I'd miss.

"You have a house in Jersey, too?" I asked, remembering the bathroom phone call. *So that's where "home" must be.*

"Yeah. Nothing major. Just a place to hide out when I need a break." Aiden paused as if something was stirring in him. "Michaela, I need to tell you something," he said, turning onto a side street to park.

I shook my head and looked out of my window. "Aiden, don't go there. Remember, Vegas?"

He placed his finger under my chin and turned my head so that I could face him.

"Okay, but I just want you to know that I missed the hell out of you. I didn't even know how much I wanted you in my life until now. When can I see you again?"

I sighed, knowing that everything he said was what I wanted, too. I just knew we both had background noise playing in our lives and if we kept going like this, we'd never be able to give ourselves fully to anyone else. I decided to be honest hoping it would help us get past this pull we had toward one another.

"Look, Aiden, I have a boyfriend," I blurted, praying it would be the ripped Band-Aid we both needed. "I mean, we're taking a break, I think. He just proposed."

"You're engaged?" he interrupted. His eyes were big and his eyebrows were furrowed.

"No, no, I'm not engaged. I wasn't, I mean, I'm not ready to be married."

He sat back in his seat as if a weight had been lifted from his shoulders.

"It doesn't matter, though," I continued. "I know the past

two days doesn't show it, but I do love him. We've been together for a while and we're just taking a break so we can figure some things out."

"So, you used me to figure yourself out?" he asked.

I shook my head. "You know that neither of us thought this would happen." I looked over to him and saw the disappointment on his face.

"You're right. I know you're right. I just wish you reached out to me sooner. Maybe things wouldn't be…" He stopped himself and sighed. "Okay, Mikki. Vegas." He nodded and put the car back in drive. His hand was back over to my side again.

We pulled up to my mother's house and he slowly walked with me to her door. He kept my hand in his, knowing these were our last few moments together but the moment my mother opened the door, Aiden freed me from his grasp.

"Hey, Mrs. D," he said, smiling like he was seventeen all over again. She looked confused as she tried to register Aiden's face. Once she realized who he was, her eyebrows rose and she engulfed him in a hug.

"Hey, baby!" She finally released him and pulled me into her arms, hugging me while shooing Rambo, her terrier-chihuahua mix.

"This dog is a mess," she said, waving us into the house. "Sit down. Aiden it's so good to see you. Do you want something to drink?" We both shook our heads and sat down on her oversized purple couch. "How's your mom? I just spoke to her a couple of weeks ago." She paused and studied our faces. "How did you two end up seeing each other?" she asked, sitting in the armchair across from us.

I sunk into one of her throw pillows leaving Aiden to answer her question.

"Well, um, we recently reconnected over Facebook and I knew she was coming home and thought I would pick her up from the airport."

"You're so sweet," she said, looking back and forth between us again.

One thing my mother wasn't, was stupid. She tilted her head and examined my face looking for *my* tell. She knew them all. I patted my lap to get Rambo's attention to use him as a distraction. He walked over to my mother and rested at her feet with a drawn-out yawn. I always hated that dog. I raised my eyes to find my mother's gaze still locked on me and without turning her head she asked, "So Aiden, how's your wife?"

The End

Nicole Bird-Faulkner is a native New Yorker who currently resides in Atlanta, GA. As a mother of four, Nicole enjoys writing the stories she can escape in. She is currently working on her next book, Games People Play, with ReShonda Tate Billingsley. www.NicoleBird-Faulkner.com.

2

TABLOID PRINCESS

By Nakecia Bowers

On the field, my husband, Jermaine Henderson had broken records with his stellar talent. But right about now, I wondered whether he had broken his vows and had me about to star in an episode of *Snapped*.

After an hour of fighting, I was worn out. I took a deep breath and tried a less violent approach.

"Give me her number right now or I'll post *your* number online," I said to my husband of eight years. I knew this threat would work because ever since he took a knee two years ago in support of Colin Kaepernick, everything he did seemed to be in the public eye and he hated it. But I didn't care. All I was thinking about was trying not to act a fool.

The catalyst behind my anger? This photo that was all up and down my timeline this morning. My husband, strolling hand-in-hand with some blonde bimbo. Well, not just *some*

14

blonde bimbo.

It wasn't just the picture that had me pissed. It was the fact that it was taken while I was out of town dealing with my grandfather's terminal illness. I had taken our six-year-old daughter with me as I often did, but I'd never had a reason not to trust my husband before.

"Baby! Calm down," he pleaded. "It looks way worse than it is. It's just the angle."

I glared as he sat on the bed. *Does he think I'm stupid?*

Her face lived in the tabloids, though I didn't know why. There were a host of D-list actresses who looked and acted better than she did. But she was tabloid fodder, ever since she'd gone through a highly publicized divorce and an ongoing child custody battle with a movie star whose name escaped me.

"You are such a liar," I shouted. "I don't want to hear anything else from you. I want to talk to her." I thrust my phone at him. "I'm waiting on the number, and I swear, if you give me a wrong number, you'll regret it."

He looked at me with sad eyes, stalling for time. He knew that hell hath no fury like me being pissed. "I'll give it to you," he said, finally. "I just want you to calm down. All of this anger can't be good for the baby."

When he said that, I touched my belly. Oh, now he remembered that I was carrying his child?

"Did you care that I was pregnant when you were taking your romantic stroll on the beach?" I snapped. "Did you care about our baby when you were spending time with that washed-up actress?" I took a deep breath, surprised that I wasn't in tears. I was too angry to cry.

"Give me her number." I held up my iPhone ready to punch-dial her digits.

My phone started vibrating and that only pissed me off more. I had turned the ringer off because ever since the photo dropped, my phone had been ringing and dinging non-stop. People kept sending me the photo, asking if I'd seen it yet.

He raised his phone that was in his lap. "I don't have her number memorized," he said.

"But you have it, right?"

He nodded, then before he could do anything else, I snatched his phone from him. I wanted her number, but anger overwhelmed me and I threw the phone back at him. He ducked; the phone missed him and crashed against the wall. He stared at me, stunned; in all of our years together, I'd never done that.

I was shocked, too, but still I said, "That's why you got traded. You can't catch." I had no clue I could be this mean. We both knew his recent trade had nothing to do with his ability; he was one of the best tight ends in the league. But his kneeling before games had gotten him traded, and his strolling with bimbos was about to have me trading him, too.

He stood, hovering over me, twisting his wedding band. I could tell that he was afraid; we'd never had it out like this. He kept his eyes on me as he slowly walked across the room to retrieve his phone.

He returned to me and held the phone up to unlock it, but before he did, I saw the shattered photo of our family on the cracked screen. He tapped in his passcode, the same as it had always been — our anniversary date. I had the same one on my phone. He scrolled through until he got to the name: Noelle Broome. I snatched the phone, but this time, I didn't throw it.

I studied her contact info: just her name and phone

number. While he sat on the bed like a scolded little boy, I airdropped the information to my phone.

He stood to speak. "Baby, I didn't-"

"One," I said, holding my finger up and counting like I did with our daughter; she knew if I got to three, she was in trouble. I was surprised it worked on him; he sat back down and shut up.

I scrolled through his text messages. With as many messages as he had, I doubted if he had deleted anything. Finally, I saw a text message from her: *I want to talk in person about that night. I keep dreaming about it.*

That was actually on his phone. If he was cheating, he was terrible at it.

"What the hell?" I shook the phone at him. "What does she keep dreaming about?" He sat confused, as if he didn't know what I was talking about. "Answer me." When he didn't say anything, I said, "I'll ask her." I didn't give him a chance to respond as I started dialing her number. The phone rang once, and then, I was sent to voicemail. Had I been thinking, I would have called from his phone. Instead of leaving a message, I sent a text:

This is Jermaine's wife. You have 15 minutes to respond or I'm sharing your phone number, the text messages and everything I know about that night to every gossip rag and blogger I can find. This is info your ex may want for your custody hearing.

I pressed 'Send' then scrolled some more through his phone and paused at a notation on his calendar. Jermaine had been searching for event coordinators for our son's baby shower.

There was silence in our bedroom. But down the hall I heard our daughter, Kennedy singing as if she was the only one in the house. I hadn't heard her sing "Let it Go" from the movie *Frozen* in a while. Did this mean something?

My phone vibrated in my hand and I read the incoming message:

It's not what it looks like. I'm in the middle of something, please give me a couple of hours.

I didn't want to give her anything, but I typed:

OK

Then, his phone vibrated and I growled when I saw the text from Noelle: *I got a message from your wife. What did you tell her?*

I responded back:

Still me. He told me the truth. Will you do the same?

She didn't text back.

*****

Time was slowly ticking while I waited for Noelle. I didn't know why I agreed to give her time to respond. Jermaine was trying to make everything as normal as possible for Kennedy as they played the piano together. He stayed away from me, trying not to upset me any more than he already had.

My teenage niece, Jas, who'd lived with us for the past few years, was somewhere in the house, on social media, I was sure. I was upstairs pacing; I couldn't settle down.

I still had Jermaine's phone and I had all the landlines in the house in the room with me. As I paced, I thought of all the memories Jermaine and I had created in this bedroom. We both loved that we'd decorated it with the calming colors of dark gray and lavender. The picture of us over the chaise lounge made me smile, but then, I finally broke down, sat on the bed and cried.

The phone vibrated and I glanced at the screen; I sighed with relief. "Hello," I said, sniffing back my tears, so glad to hear from Celia, my big sister, my rock.

"I'm glad you answered. What's going on? And before you say you're all right, turn the camera on so I can see you."

I blinked back my tears before I clicked on the camera option because I knew if I didn't, my sister would drive over here and I was not in the mood.

"I don't have answers to anything. He says it's innocent, but that's hard to believe."

"What is his side? Of the story and the pictures."

"I really haven't let him talk because I'm just so mad I want to punch him in the face. Or maybe I don't want to know the truth so that's why I'm not letting him say anything other than 'it's not what it seems.'"

"Punch him in the face? Are these pregnancy hormones talking? I've never heard you like this."

"Well, I've never had my husband cheat on me before," I said, shocked and filled with sadness to hear myself say those words.

"I have," she said matter-of-factly, but in her tone, she made her point.

Her words shut me up. My sister was once married to a football player, which was how I met Jermaine, at a team holiday party my sister and her husband hosted. I'd wanted no parts of a relationship with him or any athlete just from watching my brother-in-law. So when Jermaine asked me out, I declined, but we started hanging out as friends. It was cool, we had a lot of things in common and he was there for me when I went through a break-up. I thought Jermaine and I were going to be just a rebound relationship, but it bloomed into more than I ever imagined and after two years, he became my husband.

As Celia asked me more questions, I couldn't sit still anymore, so I opened every drawer in our bedroom to see what might have been hidden: condoms, love letters, a gift from her, there had to be something.

"Little sis, I need you to listen to me. Don't decide that you know what happened because of some photos. You're married to a man in the public eye."

This was true, though it wasn't that way when I'd married Jermaine. Back then, he was just a regular football player trying to stay on the roster. The winning Superbowl catch three years ago gave him a huge career boost. He'd turned into a household name and I had mixed feelings about it. I was happy for his success, but there was the other side. Celebrities always invited him to hang out, groupies boldly made themselves available and his name was even mentioned in a rap song.

"I know," I said, finally answering my sister. "And while I'm happy for Jermaine, I don't like when people talk about Kennedy like they know her and show up to school events for a chance to see him. I don't like people joining us at the table when we go out for dinner or knocking on our door asking for his autograph. But I was willing to deal with that; this is too much. This is humiliating. People I never talk to are texting me, trying to get in my business."

Inside his closet, I saw the sweat pants and jacket that Jermaine was wearing in the picture. I removed it from the hanger, and then did the same to everything on one side of his closet.

"In your heart, do you feel like he's cheating?"

"I don't know. I trusted this man with my life before these pictures surfaced. They're *holding hands* on the beach. Jermaine and I talked on the phone all day that day and he *never* mentioned the beach. I manage his calendar and somehow when he had me enter a business meeting, he didn't say 'put down have an affair'. Hell, maybe all of his business meetings are hook-ups." I couldn't stop my voice from trembling.

"Don't do this to yourself. Listen to him. In the meantime, I'm going to make some calls and get some answers for you. You know I'm good at this detective stuff because of my cheating ass husband. I just don't think Jermaine is that. Until we know for sure, put his clothes back."

I forgot that we'd been on a video call and she could see what I was doing. I said, "He better be glad I didn't set his stuff on fire."

We laughed before disconnecting.

*****

It was going on three hours since Noelle had responded to me. We'd already tucked Kennedy in for the night and Jermaine walked into the bedroom wearing his pajamas. He was pretty confident that he still lived here. He ignored his bag that I'd packed by the door. It wasn't all of his possessions, but it was symbolic. I was way too pregnant to pack up all of his stuff. But if I found out that he'd really cheated....

He'd walked in with my favorite pregnancy snack: a warm honey bun with melted butter.

"I don't want it," I said, knowing that I did.

Jermaine knew it, too, so he sat it down within my reach. "I know you don't want to hear what I have to say, so I decided to write it and you can read it when you're ready." There was sadness in his eyes when he handed me the letter.

Taking it from him, I said, "This is the whole truth? Nothing left out." I looked into his eyes. Not just looked, I stared deep into his soul. "Did you write about that night?"

He kinda nodded, then shook his head. "I shared what I could, but it's not my place to tell."

I frowned. "Not your place to tell? Hold up. You're willing to lose your marriage and family to protect her?"

He stared as if confused by the question. "It's not to protect her. It's complicated."

"Un-complicate it for me."

"All I can say is that I know something. Something that happened. Something I witnessed. I can't tell you anything else, baby, just trust me."

"Trust you? After those pictures? After her text?"

"Something triggered a bad memory for her. Something that she wanted to keep a secret, but now she's thinking that it's time to be revealed."

"Well, if she wants it revealed, then why can't you tell me?"

"Because...."

Before he could say anything else, I narrowed my eyes, "You don't trust me."

He shook his head and tears formed in his eyes. "I trust you; but you're so angry. I don't trust what you might do while you're like this. I don't want to put you in a position where you may use this...against her...someway."

My husband sat, looking at me, twisting his wedding band again. He always did that when he was nervous. The vibrating phone broke through my thoughts. The text read:

This is Noelle and my attorney is with me. How do you want to do this?

My husband was keeping her secret and she had the nerve to contact us with an attorney? Did I need one, too? I texted back:

Since you have your attorney and I don't have one handy, I'll call, and I'll be recording this for my own protection. I'm not interested in talking to your attorney, I want to talk to you. And I want the truth, good or bad.

Noelle texted back:

Fine, I will record, too.

Now that we were in agreement, I put through the video call. I wondered what kind of attorney she had who allowed me to call all the shots. On the other end, Noelle answered, though she wasn't looking at me.

"Is it recording everywhere?"

I assumed she was talking to her attorney about recording their call.

Finally, she turned to the screen and faced me. "Your husband is a good man. Something happened to me some years ago and your husband helped and when I came to town, all I wanted to do was thank him."

I frowned. It almost sounded as if she were reading a script.

"So he helped you to what? Walk? I'm trying to understand this hand holding thing on the beach."

"We weren't really holding hands; I grabbed his hand. I didn't know someone was taking pictures."

"Why would you grab my husband's hand?"

"We were talking about what had happened and it was an emotional moment. I needed...just a sense of security."

Was I supposed to be okay with this?

Now, I turned to Jermaine, who sat, staring without

emotion. He just looked at me, though his gaze was in direct line to the phone. "So, you were fine with this Jermaine? While my grandfather was in the hospital instead of being there with me, you needed to hold *her* hand to make *her* feel secure?"

"How many people now?"

My head turned back to the phone when I heard Noelle's voice. Her head was turned to the side again, as she spoke to someone (her attorney, I assumed) off camera. What were they talking about?

Jermaine took my attention away. "Baby, I was just trying to be supportive. I knew she felt vulnerable and I didn't want to add to that by pulling away."

My husband's explanation was no better than hers, and now, I felt even angrier. I stood up, hoping that would help me settle down.

"Well, I need one of you to share this secret with me. This secret that would make you hold my husband's hand as you're strolling on the beach. This secret," I turned to Jermaine, "that would make you not pull away, even though you have a wife at home."

There was silence and my anger rose to boiling.

"I'm about to put you both on blast. I'm about to share this bullshit with the seven-point-three million followers that Jermaine has on social media."

"Jermaine, please!" Noelle was pleading and on the screen I saw her fear — or was she really scared? She was an actress so I didn't know if this was real emotion.

"Look, Noelle. I really want to protect you; I'm a man of my word, but this is bad. I'm not willing to lose my family trying to keep your secret. I'll make sure it doesn't get out."

After a moment, she said, "Fine, tell her." There was a

pause before she added, "Just make sure you tell it all."

My eyes moved between the two of them. Was she threatening him? Daring him?

Now, I wasn't sure if I wanted to know and when I felt our son kick in my belly, I wondered if that was another sign.

Before I could tell Jermaine to be quiet, he said, "Years ago before you and I even met, I was at a party with your brother-in-law."

My heart pounded.

"There was all the standard stuff going on — drinking, drugs, sex. I was trying to fit in, but it wasn't my scene. So I was kinda off in a corner outside, when I heard a woman scream. No one else seemed to notice, but I ran into the house, searching the rooms. In the den, there was this guy on top of this woman. At first, I thought it was just wild sex, but then, by the look in her eyes, I knew it wasn't consensual. I grabbed the man off of her."

I covered my mouth with my hand as I imagined the scene.

Jermaine said, "The messed up thing is it was someone I knew, a man I'd looked up to. We had some words; he told me to mind my business and when I asked Noelle if she was all right, she told me...." He paused and took a deep breath. "She told me he raped her."

"Oh my, God," I whispered. I couldn't bring myself to look at the phone, to look at Noelle.

"He threatened me," Jermaine continued, "told me that I'd pay if I took a groupie's word over his."

My eyes and mouth were opened wide. Now, I forced myself to glance at the phone. I expected to see Noelle, stone faced and in tears. But she wasn't that way at all; she was patting her face, as if she was fixing her makeup. What the hell? But then, I figured this was what she did when she was nervous.

"At the time," my eyes turned back to Jermaine who kept on talking, "Noelle didn't want me to call the police, so I waited with her until her ride came. I told her my name just in case she ever went to the police and needed a witness. Then, I never heard from her or the police."

"So this was years ago?" I asked Jermaine and Noelle. This time, when I turned back to Noelle, there were tears in her eyes as she nodded.

"Over ten years ago," Jermaine said, "I almost forgot about it until the day, I got the call from Noelle, and it kinda threw me off because I had no clue why she wanted to meet me in person. I started to tell you," Jermaine continued as if it was just the two of us in the conversation, "but you had so much going on with your grandfather, and I really didn't know how this was going to play out with Noelle."

His words, his tone, I believed him. But still...I felt like there was more. Had anything else happened between them? Turning to Noelle, now, she was crying. I wondered if I should just end this here, but I needed more.

"You don't have to go into the rape," I said softly, trying to sound a little sympathetic, "but I need to know why you called my husband now."

She'd muted herself as she spoke to her attorney, before she turned back, took a deep breath, unmuted herself and then said, "Okay. For years I tried to block out everything about that night. I even changed my name and reinvented myself. But because of my circle, from time to time I ran into my rapist and I hated it; I hated him." She took a breath. "Mark Markson"

I gasped. Mark Markson. I knew him, I'd been around him.

I'd never been alone with him, but I thought of the many times I'd seen him at various events. I shuddered as I thought about what could have happened if my guard had ever been down when I'd been around him.

She continued, "I just tried to pretend it never happened. But when someone else accused him because of the Me Too movement, I thought about my daughter. And how I had to speak up, too. For her.

"But it's really scary to put myself out there with someone as powerful as Mark and before I did, I wanted to know if I still had my witness. If that guy who saved me would remember and if he'd be willing to stand up for me. When I reached out to Jermaine and he agreed to meet, he said it had to be in a public place because he was married and didn't want any misunderstandings."

I took a moment to ingest all of this. Finally, I asked Noelle, "So what will you do?" This conversation had not only softened me, but I believed them. It was a bit amazing that for the past few hours, I hated her and wanted to kill him. But now, I felt sorry for Noelle. Not only because of what she'd been through, but because of the decisions that were in front of her. It was difficult for any woman to step out and talk about her sexual assault; I couldn't imagine how hard it would be in the public eye and with someone like Mark Markson.

She stayed quiet, so I repeated, "What will you do now?"

"I'm not sure." She shook her head. "No one will believe me over Mark."

"You have to do this," I encouraged her. "You have to, like you said for your daughter."

She lowered her head and said, "I'm sorry."

I frowned. Why was she apologizing to me? Was there

more to this?

Then my niece Jas, banged on our opened bedroom door. "Auntie. Auntie."

"Jas," I said when I glanced up from the phone. "We're in the middle of something now. Give us a...."

"I know. You guys are trending," she said, rushing over to the bed were we sat.

"Trending?"

"Yeah, trending." She pushed her cell into my face. "On Twitter."

"What?" Jermaine and I said at the same time. I grabbed her phone and stared at the split screen. On one side was Noelle and her attorney, and on the other, there was me and Jermaine. There were comments from viewers at the bottom of the screen.

We were live? For everyone to see? For all to hear? The whole time?

Jermaine and I looked at each other, then turned to Noelle on the screen.

"What?" I asked.

"Why?" Jermaine asked, his voice filled with the anger that I'd been feeling.

I guessed my husband was thinking what I was. Noelle had been telling him that she didn't want anyone to know. And she'd just told me she didn't know what she was going to do.

Now, she'd put her business all out there — and ours, too. And it didn't take long for me to realize what she'd done. This was the only way she knew how to reveal her secret. This was the only way she knew how to tell the world.

"Oh, my God." Her voice trembled. "We're live? No! How did that happen? I didn't mean for our video to be live." She cried, but I knew her tears were fake. She was going to pretend that somehow, some way the video had gone live, but this was no accident.

I stared at the screen as she sobbed and my heart lurched. She'd used me and Jermaine. I wanted to be angry, but how could I be? She was a woman who needed to tell her story and this was the only way she knew how. And Jermaine had told half the story for her. She would have to be believed.

I didn't even say goodbye, I just clicked off the phone, then tossed the phone onto the bed. Jermaine's arms were around me before I could even reach for him.

Over his shoulder, I saw Jas tiptoe out of our bedroom. But Jermaine and I didn't move. We just held each other and in that moment, I thanked God for my husband and prayed because of the chaos that was bound to fill our lives now.

The End

Nakecia Bowers is a Social Worker turned writer who has been sharing her unique views on the world through storytelling for over 20 years. She likes to travel and resides near Los Angeles, California. She's currently working on multiple novel ideas to be released soon. You can follow her on Instagram @author.nakeciabowers and Twitter @nakeciabowers.

3

CRAZY FOR YOU

By Eric Jamal

For the last hour, I'd been reading, in disbelief, the one-sentence message I'd just received. An email that contained copies of other emails and pictures to back up what this claimed.

It's cute to see you in love with a woman who loves another man.

Casey. My Casey.

My eyes tore away from the email to the picture in the frame that sat on the nightstand on my side of the bed. There was only one word for my girlfriend - beautiful. But it was her intellect and quick humor that had captured my heart over a year ago. For the first time, I'd become a one-woman man.

Because of Casey.

I told every close friend, every family member, everyone, just how in love I was. I'd opened my heart to the point where

I'd been teased relentlessly.

"Really, Richard? It's about time. But uh...can you stop talking about Casey for one minute?" my friends would say.

I'd laughed whenever anyone kidded me; I could take the jokes. I was a comedy writer so laughing was my business. Plus, I didn't care what anyone said.

But now I was faced with this email and pictures that showed that while I'd given my whole heart to Casey, she was sharing hers with someone else.

I was filled with so many emotions, I was going to explode. I wasn't sure which feeling would make me blow. My anger? My hurt? Or would it be my fear of what my life would be like without her?

There was no way I could go through this alone. I needed a friend, another man who could give me a male perspective and a spiritual point of view.

Reaching for my cell, I stopped, then snatched my hand back as if I'd been bitten by a snake. I was about to call Jerry, who'd been more than my friend for the last three years, he'd been my confidant. The man who'd always given me not only good advice, but he backed it all up with scriptures. He gave me Godly counsel as my heart fell for Casey. But, I couldn't call him.

My glance traveled back to the email that I still gripped in my hand. I couldn't call Jerry because he was the man in the pictures, the man who was hugging and kissing and loving my Casey.

I was a man, so I wasn't going to cry. It was hard to hold it back, though. I wasn't the first, nor would I be the last man to be cheated on. But what I couldn't figure out was how had I missed this? How had I missed my friend with my girl? It was crazy because even though I'd been friends with Jerry, I didn't even know that he and Casey had met. Of course, he knew everything about her. I'd bragged about her beauty, how smart she was, how she made me laugh. I'd shown him tons of pictures and told him a million stories. When I'd first met Casey, Jerry had been the one who suggested I do a background check, just to make sure she was as great as I believed.

In the past, when I'd heard people say their hearts were broken, I just thought they were talking. But now, I understood. There was an ache in my chest that would never go away. Well maybe, one day it would. But until that time, life had to go on. My life would continue, but it wouldn't be the same for Jerry. Because if there was one thing I knew, it was that my friend had to die.

****

I wasn't sure which of the two confused me more — Casey or Jerry.

Jerry and I had met at a business seminar, then bonded over our similar stories of grandmothers who kept us in line even when life wasn't kind. I thought he was my boy. And Casey...from the moment I met her that day in that restaurant and we exchanged numbers...I thought she was my woman.

She had to be confused. Casey just didn't understand how much I loved her, how much we belonged together. That was why I'd been watching her for a few days. From down the street, with binoculars. I was waiting for that moment when I could show her what she meant to me. And then, that moment came.

I scooted down in my rented car, just a bit. I rented it so that Casey wouldn't notice me. But now, as I watched the Rolls turn into her driveway, a fire rose within me. This was what I planned. This was what I wanted Casey to see. But now, I wasn't sure if this was going to work.

Before Jerry even opened the door of his car, Casey had her front door open and she rushed out to greet him. As if she couldn't wait. She was greeting him and hugging him the way she was supposed to be greeting and hugging me.

When Jerry kissed her, I exploded from the car. I wasn't sure if it was my car door slamming or my pounding steps on the asphalt that made them turn to me, then step away from each other in shock.

"Richard!" They said my name together.

Jerry, though, didn't get my name all the way out of his mouth. I hit him with a right hook that made him stagger back, then fall to the ground.

"Richard!" Casey screamed as she went to assist the man who used to be my friend. "What are you doing?"

"What is wrong with you?" Jerry said as he stood. He held his hand to his mouth, but it didn't stop the blood from seeping through his fingers. "You hit me."

I raised my fists again to let him know that I was ready for round two. But Casey stepped in between us.

"What are you doing, Richard? Are you crazy?"

At that moment, I wanted to tell her that yeah, I was crazy — crazy in love with her. But not only did I not want to appear insane, but I was too mad to speak.

"What is wrong with you?" Jerry bucked up to me.

"You need to step back," I said, speaking my first words. "And then tell me why you're a lying, stealing, backstabbing friend. You know you're wrong for this." I dropped my hands and looked between the two of them. "She's my woman."

The smirk that filled his face made me want to punch him again. He was looking at me as if I were a punk.

"You know you're wrong," I shouted.

He sucked on blood seeping from his busted lip. "I can have you arrested for attacking me."

"Go ahead." I raised my hands high. "Call the police."

"No, Jerry," Casey said. She placed her hand on my chest to stop me from moving, but she spoke to him. "Can you please go inside? I need to talk to Richard."

"I'm not leaving you out here with him."

I wanted to punch him again for saying that, but Casey must've had a hold over him the same way she had a hold over me. She gave him a look and he stepped away. But not before he stared me down, then leaned over to give Casey a kiss.

My fingers clutched into a fist, but Casey turned her head making him miss her lips. But finally, we were alone and Casey faced me.

"You shouldn't have done that," she said.

"I could say the same about you." I swallowed back my tears and manned up. "Why, Casey?"

She sighed as if she was tired.

I'd come over here to show Casey what I was willing to do for her. I wanted to show her that I would fight for her. It didn't matter that she had been keeping secrets and telling lies. I was willing to forgive, but it didn't seem as if she was impressed with what I'd done.

She said, "I didn't mean for it to go down this way."

"Which way did you want it to go down?"

"I don't know," she said, looking away from me. "I needed

a little space."

"From me?"

Now, she looked up and nodded.

"Space from me with him?"

She shrugged. "It's just that I think he's more suitable for me."

What was that supposed to mean? Since she was standing right there, I could've asked her, but I felt like a complete idiot. Or maybe I was just confused because Casey was making me feel like I was the only one who'd been in our relationship. She was downplaying what we had because I thought we were more than suitable for each other; we were in love.

Staring at her, all I could do was shake my head. I had completely misread her and she could have told me instead of having me find out through some anonymous email.

"Richard, are you okay?"

I guess the way I was staring blankly made her ask me that. But I didn't have anything else to say. So, I just turned around and walked away.

****

I was out of control. For a week, it felt like I'd only been doing two things: at home, staring at the email or out in my car, following Jerry and Casey around Los Angeles.

This time, I was in my car, not even caring if the two of them saw me, though they never did. They seemed to only have eyes for each other.

I caught a glimpse of Casey and Jerry every day and every time, Casey looked more beautiful. She was the same woman I'd fallen in love with, so I couldn't believe she hadn't figured out yet that Jerry was a liar and a fake. I knew what had drawn Casey to Jerry. He played himself off as a Godly man. But now, I knew the truth about him — he was a man who used his success and fake religion to lure women. If he did this to me, I knew he'd done it to others. He would never be faithful to Casey.

Leaving my office, my car almost navigated itself to Casey's house, but tonight, there wasn't a car in the driveway and my fists clenched. I knew what that meant. Trying not to break speed limits, I made my way over to Jerry's easing through the streets of Inglewood. About twenty minutes later, I slowed my car as I approached Jerry's street, then stopped in front of his house. Inside, the lights were on, even though there wasn't a car in the driveway. But I knew the reason for that.

Easing my car around to the back, I saw his Rolls Royce where he'd always parked it. Turning off my lights, I pulled over to the other side of the street. I opened my glove compartment and pulled out my gun, a Glock 26, 9mm. The darkness was my cover as I trotted toward the car, my rubber bottom shoes, silent against the asphalt.

I stopped just feet beside his car and for a moment, thought about all the times that I'd confided in Jerry about everything. And he'd taken that and used it against me. He'd taken all that I'd told him and used it to steal my woman. I raised the gun, then unloaded the chamber into the Rolls. There was a silencer on the gun, but not on the bullets that pelted against the car. I wanted to take a few seconds to admire the gift I was leaving for Jerry, but I didn't have much time before people looked out their windows or maybe even came onto the street. So, I jumped into my car, and drove away, mindful to stay within the speed limits so I wouldn't draw attention to myself.

I wished I could be there to see Jerry's face when he discovered what happened to his precious car. The only thing — I wished he knew it was me. He would never think that, though, because it was so out of character for me – even with him stealing my woman. He'd blame this on random vandals. But that was best, I guessed. I didn't need to be in jail.

I did feel better though. Tonight, it was just a car and I wondered what tomorrow would bring.

****

I couldn't believe I had actually convinced Casey to meet me and as I sat in the coffee shop, I wondered if she had told Jerry that she was meeting me. And if she told him, was he worried? Did he think I would be able to win her back?

I wasn't sure if that was his question, but it was mine. Because even though weeks had passed, I still couldn't bring myself to let it go. It was like there was a mental hold on my heart and my good sense. Maybe because I couldn't understand this. I was the man women fought for, the man women worked hard to get to settle down. I still couldn't wrap my head around the fact that Casey had gotten distracted by Mr. 6'5", dark, and conniving.

All of those thoughts went out of my head when Casey walked in looking like a goddess. Her jeans alone made me forget that I'd been dumped.

"Hey, Richard," she said sweetly as she hugged me.

I inhaled; she smelled like heaven and her hug felt like foreplay. I hated when she pulled away.

"Do you want something to drink, something to eat?" I

asked, pointing to the counter.

She shook her head. "I really don't have much time," she said. "Let's talk."

I nodded, and waited until she sat before I did the same. She started talking, but for a few moments, I heard nothing. Just stared at her lips. I was mesmerized until I interrupted her. "I'm sorry, can you repeat what you just said."

"Okay." She frowned. "But why?"

"Because I was distracted by your beauty."

Her smirk turned into a smile. "You're such a charmer. I see why all the ladies love you."

"Why don't you love me?"

She laughed and though I thought that was odd, I didn't say anything. She said, "It wasn't that I didn't want to love you, it was that dating you made me realize two things: what I wanted and what you really needed in your life for the long haul."

These didn't even sound like her words. It was Jerry who'd tainted her mind against me. But, I wasn't going to spend our time talking about him. So, I said, "You're what I need for the long haul. Don't you know you're my diamond that shines?"

When she laughed again, it dawned on me that she thought I was joking.

She touched my hand. "Richard, this is what I know — you're going to make some woman very happy when you're ready to settle down and be a one-woman man."

I didn't know why she didn't know how I felt about her. I smiled in hopes that she would be able to see my sincerity. "I'm already a one-woman man. It's only been you for this past year."

She laughed again and now, I was beginning to get a

complex. I enjoyed a good joke as much as the next person since humor was my job, but right now, I was serious. I wanted my woman back and it appeared that we were having two different conversations. Hers was funny, mine was not.

I didn't get a chance to get us on track because she glanced down at her watch. "I've got to get going." It felt abrupt to me, she'd just gotten here. But when she stood, I stood with her and she hugged me again. "Take care. I'll see you around."

I stood like a statue as she sauntered out of the coffee shop. There was still so much I wanted to say; she didn't give me enough time.

But Casey was right about one thing — she would see me around, maybe sooner than she thought.

****

I'd always thought of myself as a normal guy, having a blessed, but normal life. But since I'd found out about Casey and Jerry, I'd become a man I didn't recognize. I made my way to work every day, somehow ate two maybe three meals. But my time and my focus was on Casey and Jerry. I followed them whenever I could find them.

Today, they were down at the Santa Monica pier and through my binoculars, I watched them as they held hands and laughed together. Seeing them like this still lit a fire within me and made me wonder what was I doing? Why was I torturing myself this way? It was because of Jerry — this was a betrayal that I couldn't get over.

As they headed back toward me, I lowered the binoculars and closed my eyes. I'd been hoping that by now Casey and I would be back on, but how would that happened when they were always together, always laughing, always having fun....

The knock on my window startled me, made me sit up straight. I pushed the door open and stepped out. Jerry stood right behind her and while he wore a look of disgust, the expression on her face didn't tell me anything. I wasn't sure if she was angry or what. But what I did notice was a little scratch on the side of her face. What was that? Was Jerry beating her? For a moment, my eyes went to his and I wanted to hit him again. If he was hurting her....

"What are you doing, Richard?" she asked, bringing my attention back to her. "Are you following us now?"

"Why would I follow you?" I asked, but before she could answer, I said, "You're beautiful."

"What? Richard, this is crazy, you know that, right?"

I shook my head. "It's not. I can rescue you."

Her eyes squinted in confusion. "Rescue me from what?"

My eyes went from hers to Jerry's and he just stared back, pitifully. I didn't care what he thought, but I was sorry he was here. She wouldn't tell me what was going on behind their closed doors. If there had been any way, I would have set up cameras in her home and his. But that would've been a little crazy.

"Richard," she said, shifting from one foot to the other, "you have to stop this and if you don't, we'll get a restraining order."

My eyebrows rose. "It's we now? He's gotten into your head, I see."

She sighed and everything on her face softened. She gave me a half smile as she reached for my hand.

I glanced up at Jerry, but he didn't move. So I tightened my fingers around hers.

She said, "You know I really care about you, right? You've been a great friend and you're a sensitive, loving man. But I think...you need help."

My eyes narrowed. What was she trying to say?

"What's going on here," she continued, "it's no longer funny. It's not flattering. And I'm becoming concerned."

"Why?"

She pressed her lips together, at first. But then, she added, "You're not trying to move on. What we had was good while it lasted, and I hope that your next relationship will blossom to something more."

Her words let me know I just hadn't been clear enough. She didn't understand, but I'd figure it out. I'd find a way to make her know just how much I loved her.

I squeezed her hand, then got back inside my car. I revved up the engine and edged away from the curb without looking back at either one of them. But not even a minute passed before I wanted to turn back around. Casey just didn't get it. Clearly, there was something wrong with our communication, and I needed to fix that.

Nodding my head, I knew what I had to do.

****

It felt like I'd been waiting for hours for Casey to come home. My bet was that she'd be alone. That had been their pattern over the last few weeks; Casey came home alone on Sunday nights.

I didn't care how long I had to wait, even though the hour was approaching midnight. Because I had to get her to understand how I felt and get her to realize that Jerry was more than a liar, he was a snake, especially if he was putting his hands on her. I couldn't stop thinking about the scratch on her face. If that man was beating her, I was going to beat him until he wasn't breathing anymore.

The lights of an approaching car made me sit up and as it slowed, I smiled. But then, I frowned. It wasn't Casey's Altima.

Jerry jumped out of his Rolls, already screaming. "What the hell are you doing here?"

Casey slid out from the passenger side, but this time, she said nothing to me. I guessed she was going to let Jerry handle this.

But, I didn't want to talk to him. "Casey," I called out to her. "What do you want me to do? What do I have to do to prove to you how much I love you."

She sighed.

"I have to show you," I shouted to her. "What do you want? Should I kill him now?"

Jerry leaned his head back and laughed, a hollow sound that filled the dark of the night. "You play too much," he said when he got himself together. "You're gonna kill me?"

It was the expression on my face that took his laughter away.

"Well," he pulled out his cell from his pocket. "I'm calling the police because this time, you've gone too far."

Before he had time to awaken his screen, I gave him another hook and was surprised when I connected. I couldn't believe he left himself open like that to me when I'd done it before.

But this time, I didn't stop. I kept hitting him until he fell to the ground.

"Stop it," Casey screamed.

Neither one of us did what she asked. Jerry hit me back, but he wasn't connecting. I beat him with all of the emotions that had built up inside of me. I beat him for being a liar, I beat him for pretending and using the Lord's name in vain. And I beat him for putting his hands on Casey.

Now, she'd see how much I loved her.

As Jerry and I battled it out on the ground, I heard Casey's screams above us, but nothing was going to stop me. Not until Jerry was....

Then, a glimmer, the tip of a knife. Where had that come from? I leaned back.

"Yeah, you better get off me," Jerry growled as he wielded the knife toward me.

His face was so bloody, I hardly recognized him.

"Oh my, God," Casey cried out, but she didn't move, she stayed behind me as if she knew I'd protect her.

"You're going to be sorry you ever came after me." Jerry stumbled across the driveway.

At first, I didn't know what he was doing, but then, I realized he was searching for his phone. It must have been the beating I'd just given him. Because he couldn't have been thinking when he lowered his eyes and his hand and the knife.

I twisted, then gave him a side kick that sent him and the knife flying in the air. There were screams, but my focus was only on the knife. I grabbed it before it hit the ground and turned back to Jerry. Again, he must've been delirious, the way he charged me.

But I was ready for him. With the knife in my hand. From where I stood, I could see Casey's face, a mixture of shock and horror. I hoped that she could see my expression, my love for her.

That was my thought when I jabbed the knife into the middle of Jerry's chest.

The End

Eric Jamal *is a poet, avid reader and storyteller. He's currently working on his first full novel. He also writes songs and uses his musical knowledge to breathe life into the stories and songs that he writes.*

4

TRENDY LIES

By Candice Y. Johnson

If I had to do it all over again…I'd still whip that heifer's tail.

"You can't fight a pregnant woman Corrine," my friend Larissa screamed my name as she lodged herself between me and the backstabbing life coach I called my mentor – Sparkle Rose Langston. The three of us wrestled our way under the pink and blue balloon arch mounted at the front of Sparkle's gargantuan back yard, and tore through the *FOOTBALL OR TUTU?* banner mounted by the sandwich buffet. The banner was ugly, anyway.

"Do you know how hard I worked designing that thing," Larissa shrieked. She struggled her hardest to pull me off Mommy Dearest, who strained to get loose from my grasp.

"Bill me for it," I spat – along with a slew of four letter words. The shocked partygoers gasped in unison, like they didn't use those words themselves. Regularly.

I'm certain cussing out the guest of honor with a handful of her hair wrapped around my fingers wasn't the way anyone expected this gender reveal party to end, yet here we were. Larissa attempted to separate us again, but the auburn lacefront stuck to Sparkle's head like it was superglued. Normally, I'm not a fighter. Especially women with child. But in this case, an exception was necessary. This demon deserved to lose a patch of hair; she was pregnant by my man.

"Corrine please stop," Larissa pleaded, out of breath. "You'll never forgive yourself for this."

"I'm pressing charges," Sparkle yelped, digging her sharp acrylics into my hand. I didn't care if she drew blood, there was no way I was letting go.

"You're pregnant by my fiancé, witch. Nobody will convict me."

"Would you feel better if my baby wasn't Max's?"

Sparkle's question forced my hand open. Her long tresses slipped through my fingers as I backed away, panting. Beads of sweat trickled into my eyes. Either that or I was crying. Hearing Sparkle confirm what I already knew was true burned worse than the sun blaring on my bare arms. I sowed my dreams, hope and loads of money into this heifer, who had zero guilt admitting the seed she carried was not her husband's. I didn't care that I spoiled the gender reveal. Sparkle spoiled my life.

"I hate you!" I lunged for Sparkle again, but Larissa summoned the strength to hold me back. Sparkle stumbled, regained her pristine composure and patted her rotund belly.

"Let me at that old poached-egged demon," I hissed.

"Well this *old poached-egged demon's* womb worked well enough to scramble Max's little soldiers didn't it, Corrine?"

Sparkle winked. "But you wouldn't know that, huh?"

Sparkle talked a mouth full of noise for a woman seconds from discovering how black really feels when it's beaten off a bare butt. I wiped my face with the back of my hand, exhausted. Leave it to Sparkle to pick a day hotter than the devil's crack to throw an outdoor party. The unbearable heat made it feel like we'd been fighting an entire work day when in reality, it had only been fifteen minutes.

See, Sparkle's assistant Anita left a tray of cupcakes in the house, so I ran back inside to get it. That's when I overheard the junior ballerina Sparkle hired to dance the baby's gender with coordinating ribbons on the phone telling someone that she saw Max - my Max, canoodling with the 40-something freak. She said they bragged how he knocked her up instead of Trey, Sparkle's husband, and had gotten over on us. Even called me stupid. Once I heard enough, I dropped the cupcakes on the floor and marched right outside, swinging on Sparkle, no questions asked. Sparkle's husband stood next to the overpriced four-tier chocolate cake, mouth wide open, looking just as bewildered as me. Rather than helping Sparkle, Trey teared up like he didn't want the training wheels taken off his tricycle.

"...by the way, it's a girl," she said.

"I'm going to rip your face off," I warned Sparkle.

"Stop it. They've got their phones up." Anita - Sparkle's brainwashed right hand at *You Can Have It All International,* admonished through clenched teeth. She nodded to partygoers pointing their devices at me and Sparkle.

Larissa tapped me on the shoulder. "Anita's right, Corrine. You want to go viral for the wrong reasons?"

"I know I'm right," Anita snapped. "Corrine, you and

Sparkle are two grown, beautiful black women. Control yourselves and show it."

"Correction," I said. "Sparkle is a beautiful black bi-"

"Watch your mouth," Sparkle hissed.

"Watch your back," I snapped.

"Can you show some decorum?" Anita shoved her hands on her thin hips.

"Can you remove your lips from Sparkle's behind long enough to admit this is foul, Anita?" I snarled. "Don't be deceived thinking she's going to help you come up. Your back is the next to get a knife in it."

"Calm down Corrine, please." Larissa raised her voice above ours. "Do you hear what these people around you are saying?"

"Is Sparkle all right?"

"How could Corrine choke a pregnant woman?"

"Girl, this is some project stuff."

The crowd audibly pitied my ghetto behavior, ignoring the pain Sparkle caused me. How was the harlot the victim? No one – not a soul, asked if I was okay. Forget Sparkle. She could go to hell.

I mean, look at me: I was young, fine as a dime, still owned my own eyebrows and teeth, my design company operated in the black after only six months of existence and swelled to seven figures almost overnight. I was funny, chic and relatively level-headed until the witch I paid to level-up my business penciled letting my man *punch the kitten* in the fine print of our contract.

Y'all know what I mean.

"Corrine, I think it's best if you go home." Trey finally found the gumption to speak. His tone was low, calm. Nothing like a man who just found out he may need tickets to *The Maury Show* to find out if he was indeed the father. The sun performed a salsa with the specs of red and gray sprouting from his head. The tiny mole on his right cheek flipped me off. His sunken eyes issued a warrant for my arrest. I hadn't considered Trey. How this revelation could destroy him, too. Too bad his trifling wife hadn't thought about me.

"I'm not going anywhere, Trey. And if you had any sense at all, you'd check your wife instead of me, idiot." My anger was misplaced, cruel and unnecessary. But we've all fallen victim to friendly fire a time or two in our lives.

Sorry, Trey. You should have ducked.

"Stay here acting a fool if you want to, Corrine." Trey remained calm. "I'm going to clear my head."

He started making his grand exit across the manicured backyard, but spun abruptly on his heels when he reached the pool. "At least you didn't marry Max. The Lord saved you from the fate I'm suffering now."

My pride littered the ground as Trey walked away. I didn't care if Max and I hadn't made it down the aisle; this situation was unfair and completely went against my life plan and vision board.

The vision Sparkle helped me create.

With my mentor hurling insults at my back, I strolled up the cement path leading to the exit, pausing by the pool. I stared at my reflection in the blue water, knowing I wasn't leaving Sparkle's house. Not without some semblance of satisfaction. Not necessarily a bloodbath (or anything that could cop me a good ten-to-life), but something had to be ripped, shredded, tore up, disfigured, rearranged ...*something*, before I went home to deal with Max.

I stepped out of the brown wedges that pinched my toes since this debacle jumped off, and secured the straps of my yellow sundress. I bat my lashes like I was courting a first date, and braced for Sparkle, her entourage, and the rest of the guests charging toward me. I adjusted my hoop earrings and smoothed the sides of my high ponytail. Despite the earlier demonstration, I was still a lady. A lady prepared to bring clarity to this misunderstanding.

"You promised you'd help me get to the next level." I pointed a finger in Sparkle's face.

"Well I did, didn't I?" Sparkle jammed her hands on her hips. "*Positively Dressed* wouldn't be where it is today if I hadn't helped you."

"Yes, but the problem is you helped yourself to my man in the process."

"Don't be a child, Corrine. Max helped himself to me." Sparkle had the nerve to rest her hands on my shoulders, speaking in the same monotone voice she used on her coaching clients. "Men aren't stolen, honey - they're gifted by foolish women who fail to satisfy them to those who can."

I silently rebuked the devil and knocked Sparkle's hands away. Her breath smelled like buttercream icing, though her words reeked of sewage. My eyes scanned the length of her tall frame, before landing on her green eyes.

How could I surrender my mental health to this snake?

Sparkle's present was assassinating my future.

"You don't have to speak to her that way, Sparkle." Larissa came to my defense.

"Get real, Larissa." Sparkle took her hands off me and folded her arms. "I took you from thrift stores and dumpster diving to six figures a month, Corrine. Where's the gratitude?"

"I got your gratitude right here." I waved my shoes in Sparkle's face.

"Whatever," Sparkle brushed my hand away. "Point is, I made you successful. Max is an added perk."

If I could have swiped those uneven brows off that psycho's face with my fists, I would have got to blotting. "I thought we were friends, Sparkle?"

"Yes well, you thought your fiancé was the only one sleeping in your bed, too."

Ouch.

"What's the first thing I taught you, Corrine?" Sparkle asked.

I fumbled through my mental files before recalling Coach Sparkle's number one command. "BOSS women keep it real with themselves," I mumbled. "We're told enough lies without telling ourselves the truth."

"Good. At least you paid attention to something I taught you." Sparkle applauded in my face. "Now admit you already knew you're not the only woman Max is screwing." Sparkle brushed stray hairs sticking to her moist face, then held up two fingers. "Rule two: make sure your man's work hours match his paychecks, honey."

"Oh my God," my voice cracked.

"That's right, Corrine. I was Max's overtime. Time he made up to avoid spending with you."

"Oooooo," the crowd collectively gasped. Some laughed while others shook their heads in pity for me. I needed a hug.

Sparkle and I stared each other down. My mind raced back to the day I came across one of her videos on social media, urging women to quit corporate bondage and live their best entrepreneurial lives. Her huge following and proven results of

51

her own journey to wealth made me reach out to her for help. I was barely making enough money at my call center job to pay for Sparkle's services, but that didn't stop her from taking me under her care.

"Don't worry about the money," Sparkle assured me. "I see something special in you. One day you'll pay me back."

Sparkle was right.

I was special. And every deed she'd done to me was most certainly going to be *specially* paid back, until I took her down and got rich off her misery.

Larissa gently took my hand in hers. "We should go, Corrine." She shook her head at Sparkle. We've all had enough for today."

I nodded in silence, bent down and slid my shoes on. I scanned the cluster of shell-shocked guests, wondering how much of my breakdown they caught on video. This was the last thing I needed to show up on social media. As bad as I wanted to disappear and return to the land of faithfulness and monogamy, I didn't regret anything except not snatching Sparkle's wig all the way off. That and the demon seed she produced. Wait - that's not fair. It wasn't the baby's fault she had trifling, conniving parents. The baby was as much a victim of their flesh as I was. I had more questions than answers. Was more hurt than pissed. But I was ready to toe-tag my engagement and get on with my life. After I murdered Max.

I strolled up the graveled walkway, determined to hang onto what remained of my dignity. Sparkle chattered on and on. Putting the blame on me, toying with my patience and testing my ignorance level. The last series of insults picked at my scabs. I had enough. I doubled back to where Sparkle taunted me, poolside.

Lord, forgive me…and protect the baby, I thought as I casually shoved Sparkle into the pool and raced to my car.

*****

I can't believe you played yourself, Corrine.

I sat in my driveway, licking my self-inflicted wounds. Stored up tears coursed through my mascara, streaking my face with more animosity than I had for my betrayers.

I looked like what the heck I'd been through.

My phone chimed for the hundredth time since pulling into my driveway, but I didn't have the strength to navigate through the notifications. Most of them were social media, sharing footage of the fight. Some folk sided with me, others with Sparkle. But the consensus was we were both a mess and disgrace to Black women. Either way, I was too in my feelings to keep scrolling.

I sucked back the snot sliding from my nostrils, thinking of returning one of Larissa's back-to-back calls. She'd been blowing up my cell since I sped from Sparkle's driveway, but I rejected every call. In so many ways, Larissa was my twin canvas - right down to our cheating men. When she discovered her ex-husband Joseph was humping every pair of spread legs south of the Mississippi River, we cried together, gorged, cussed, and cried some more before Larissa took her wealthy ex to court to find out if money did indeed buy happiness.

According to her - it did.

Following the divorce, Larissa became a self-proclaimed *Cheat Whisperer,* sniffing out trysts, liaisons and secret rendezvous on a bed of lies and Trojans. She made blowing up unfaithful men her mission, so I blew it off when I thought she wrongfully targeted mine.

"I'm telling you, Corrine. You better watch Max more closely," Larissa warned me over Sushi - a month before Sparkle's gender reveal. "Just because you said yes to monogamy, doesn't mean Max has."

I fished bits of sesame from my teeth before answering, "Girl, please. All men aren't dogs. Joseph's infidelity doesn't mean Max is out here in these streets doing dirt, too."

"Mark my words, Boo." Larissa took a long sip of wine. "I'm not hating on love. It's just that I see heartbreak bear its teeth before it bites. You better watch."

"Check please," I told the waiter.

Now my blissful ignorance was being cashed in.

My cell bounced on my lap again. Checking the screen, it was the one person I couldn't ignore.

"I'll kill him!" the heavy male voice roared through the phone.

"And hello to you too, Daddy." More tears slid down my cheeks. Daddy was my confidante. He would know how to fix this mess.

"Your mother showed me the video, Baby Girl. I'm on my way." Daddy was a retired Marine. Big. Burly. No nonsense. Would duel to the death for his faith and his family. But right now I didn't need a savior. I just needed Daddy.

"It's all right, Daddy. You don't have to come. Max isn't here, anyway."

"I don't care if that boy's there. I'm coming to check on my baby."

"I'm not okay but I'll be fine, Dad. You taught me how to bounce back when I fall. I just need to man up and get through it."

Daddy sighed. "Don't worry about manning up, soldier. You have permission to own your heartbreak. You just can't stay there."

More tears.

A few minutes of them actually. I couldn't use my words because my chest was flooded with mucus. Daddy just let me cry until I couldn't squeeze out any more tears. Now I wished I'd let him come on over.

"You good?" he finally interrupted my blubbering.

"No sir. But I will be." Daddy raised me to respect myself enough to demand respect from men. He showed me how a woman should be treated. What to *require*, not *request*. Drilled in me that I should never settle, to bring my best to the table and expect the best in return. I had to give it to Max. At least he'd already given me the best of the worst.

"I'm going to give you your space," Daddy interrupted my thoughts, "but tomorrow we go to lunch." He knew for me, food made everything better. At least for the moment.

"Sure, Daddy. It's a date."

"And if Max shows up tonight, you tell that son-of-a-"

"I gotta go, Daddy." I didn't want him going off on another tangent. "Tell Mom I'm okay."

"Oh, shoot. We better pray Sparkle is okay," Daddy sheepishly said.

"Sparkle? Why?"

"Your mother headed over to her house about thirty minutes ago."

"Bye, Daddy."

I dug a tissue from my purse and blew into it. I cleaned my nose, thinking of meeting Max, fresh out of college. The way he wooed me. My stupid swooning in response. The nights I treated him like a king. The days my good make-up was wasted because he stood me up. I recalled the day we moved in together; how determined I was to hold on to this man despite everyone's warnings, until we shared the same last name.

Two hours I sat in my SUV, mentally checking receipts of every time I granted my mentor and my man multiple opportunities to hook up.

"Oh my God," I wailed. "I made it so easy for them."

I fished a mini chocolate bar from the front compartment of my purse, ripped the wrapping off and inhaled that sucker in less than thirty seconds. It tasted stale. Nothing would taste good until I had answers and reparations.

I sat there so long, cramps shot up both my legs. It was time to get out of the car, and face the world outside my four-wheeled comforter. I planned to answer a call or two. Maybe even work my way up to laughing about this later. But for now, I just wanted my bed. The bed love used to sleep in.

I took a few minutes to fix my face and look like a presentable human being, then opened the door, slid off the front seat and willed my feet to move. Once they touched the concrete, I threw my purse over my shoulder, shut the door and set the alarm.

I was halfway to the front door of my house when it flew open. Trey - *Sparkle's* Trey, stepped outside to greet me. Arms open. The biggest grin on his face. I dropped my things on the ground, fell into his arms and let his mouth take control of mine. We stood in the open, like teenagers who couldn't get enough of each other.

…we never could.

"So I guess we're free now, huh?" Trey slid his hands down my back.

"I guess we are," I answered with another kiss. I rested my head on his chest, inhaling the scent I'd come to ravish over the last year. "I never thought Max and Sparkle would be bold enough to have a baby together."

"Good for them," Trey said. "Now we can start working on our own."

The End

Candice "Ordered Steps" Johnson *spins stories of love, loss and overwhelming faith. Her creativity isn't simply hidden between the pages; she's an Emmy-winning choreographer, dancer and filmmaker who uses art to survive. Practice What You Praise (which is also a short film), Only Tithes Will Tell and Catching Feelings for Christmas are but a few of her titles. She wears her heart on her pen and hangs hope in creating. Connecting is her passion & she'd love to hear from you: candiceosp@gmail.com.*

5

HIS FIRST LOVE, HIS FIRST LADY

By Sherron Elise

"Guess who's the keynote speaker for the church's anniversary ceremony next month?"

Kara Steepleton rolled her eyes. Why couldn't her mother just come out with it? Trying hard to hide her exasperation, Kara played along. "Who?"

"Matthew and his lovely wife, Madison, will be our guests," Lorna Steepleton announced.

Kara nearly dropped her Android as if it had suddenly exploded. "Mom, please tell me you didn't!" Kara exclaimed. She could hardly believe this and now she regretted showing her mother Matthew's Facebook profile when she'd gone digging online for the whereabouts of her high school and college sweetheart.

Kara had dated Matthew Harding in high school and they'd attended Hampton University together. But their relationship came to a crossroads when Kara refused to follow him to Alabama after graduation. Matthew had landed a great career opportunity with an engineering company. The idea of living in Alabama didn't appeal to Kara. Not only that, but Matthew hadn't even proposed. She wasn't willing to uproot her life to simply play house. The fact that Matthew seemed reluctant to marry her solidified her decision to walk away. So she returned to their hometown of Houston and used her business degree to establish a lucrative career in the oil and gas industry. The couple that was once so in love had not been in contact with one another for over eight years. For Kara, once a relationship was over, then it was a wrap. No U-turns. He was your ex for a reason and if it was meant to be, then it would've worked out.

Still, a part of her was hurt that Matthew hadn't attempted to reach out to her either. It made Kara second-guess the validity of their relationship and reason it was just young and silly puppy love.

An afternoon of boredom caused her to do some cyber-sleuthing and look him up online. She wasn't really surprised to discover he was married to some woman he'd met in Alabama and the father of two little boys. But what did surprise her was the fact that he was now a minister. Matthew wasn't very religious throughout their years of dating. This was another reason Kara found it easy to part ways with him because it was apparent they were unequally yoked. Kara was the daughter of a Bishop, though her relationship with Matthew was anything but pure. She took their breakup as a sign that he wasn't God's best for her. So discovering he was now a Pastor was appalling. He'd left the engineering field to move back to Houston and pursue ministry full-time, founding his own church. Kara had spent over an hour looking through the Facebook pages of both he and his wife before jealousy caused her to log off.

Just where had this ministerial aspiration come from? And why hadn't Matthew sought *her* out once he'd turned his life around for Christ? Didn't he think she'd be the perfect first lady?

Kara considered saying hello through Facebook Messenger but she did have her pride. After all this time, why hadn't he attempted to reach out to her? But Kara made the mistake of filling her mother in on the new Pastor Matthew Harding. And Lady Steepleton had taken it upon herself to extend an invitation to him to speak at their church's most exclusive ceremony.

"So, did he ask anything about me?" Kara asked her mother.

Lady Lorna chuckled. "I was waiting on this question. Yes, of course he did."

"Wait…you didn't tell him I was still single, did you?"

"No, I didn't mention anything about your dating life. I just told him you were an oil and gas executive," Lorna replied.

Kara was satisfied with that. At least Matthew was aware she had it going on better than his frumpy looking *housewife*, which was what Madison had placed as her occupation on her Facebook page.

Something else was bothering Kara, though. "Mom, when did you talk to Matthew about the church anniversary?"

"A couple of months ago. I wanted to make sure he had

adequate notice. I know how busy church pastors can be."

And yet Matthew still hadn't tried to contact her. Why hadn't he informed her he would be coming to her church? The same church she used to have to practically drag him to come and visit while they were dating?

Well, she'd show him. The church anniversary was next month and Kara wanted to make sure she looked breathtaking. Once the ceremony was over, Kara wanted it to be clear to Matthew that he'd chosen the wrong woman to be his First Lady.

****

The Sunday of Holy Ground Tabernacle's 25th church anniversary had arrived and Kara was like Beyoncé, in formation and ready! She wore a salmon colored Ben Marc three-piece skirt suit with embroidered diamonds along the lapel of her jacket and her hat. Honestly, Kara couldn't stand wearing those gaudy church hats. They'd always seemed so matronly, but she wanted to go all out for this occasion. She suppressed a smirk at how some of the members did double-takes when she stepped into the church's vestibule, prepared to walk into the church with her parents for their grand entrance. It was here that she came face-to-face with Matthew Harding after eight long years.

"Kara! Praise God, it's so good to see you, my sister," Matthew said, still looking like a young Blair Underwood and giving Kara what she deemed as a friendly hug. He gently pulled Fran-the-Frump forward and made introductions.

"This is my beautiful wife, Madison. Baby, this is Kara, my good friend from high school and college."

Madison extended her hand. "God bless you, Kara. It's a pleasure to meet you," she said, flashing a huge smile.

Kara grudgingly had to admit that even though Madison was on the plain and mousy looking side, she was still kind of cute. She just needed more makeup to accentuate her banana pudding skin tone instead of the simple lip-gloss and light blush she was wearing. Miss Madison also needed a wardrobe consultant ASAP. She was dressed in a black sheath dress and pearls, as if Matthew was officiating a funeral instead of a church anniversary.

Kara played nice and graciously greeted and welcomed them both. But inside she was seething. How dare Matthew downplay their relationship? Introducing her as a good friend? He had taken her virginity. He was her first love!

Matthew's blasé attitude only fueled the fire for her to put on quite a show during the ceremony. Kara possessed a beautiful voice and was already a standout in the church choir but that afternoon she was on a ten. She sang *"I Get Joy When I Think About What He's Done for Me"* at the top of her lungs, even coming down from the choir stand and doing a little holy dance in front of the pulpit. She then made her way up and down the aisles, placing the mic in front of different members to get them to sing along. Once the song was finished she walked back into the choir stand, waving her hand in praise and fanning herself with her hat. She made sure to avoid her parents' eyes, knowing they were aware that she was merely showing off for Matthew. If Kara knew her father, the Great Bishop was not pleased.

Yet her shenanigans didn't stop there. Kara continued to make a point of being seen throughout the duration of the service. She led the collection of the offering, even though that was clearly a task relegated to the finance committee. During her tribute speech to her parents she teared up and thanked them for molding her into a dedicated servant of God, rattling off all the ministries she was involved in. When Matthew finally took the podium, Kara stood with the NLT version of the Bible on her Kindle, ready to read the scriptures aloud for him as he preached.

"Kara, I know you are on fire for God but I usually have my wife read for me when I'm ministering," Matthew said with a grin.

Light laughter sounded throughout the congregation and Kara, thoroughly embarrassed, apologized and took her seat. But she chimed in plenty of 'amens' and 'hallelujahs' during Matthew's sermon, which she had to admit was pretty good. God had truly transformed him into a dynamic preacher. This reaffirmed Kara's conviction that he was more deserving of a wife such as herself.

She noted that Madison was not a very vocal first lady. She sat in her seat and clapped along to the music, amen-ing at all the right times, but it seemed as if she preferred to keep a low profile. Even as she read the scriptures her voice seemed quivery and unsteady.

After the service, Kara approached Madison in the fellowship hall during dinner to apologize for the scripture reading mishap.

"I usually read the scriptures for my Father," Kara lied as a form of explanation. Her mother read for her father each Sunday.

Madison smiled and gave her a hug. "No offense taken. I really enjoyed the service. You have so much energy. I'm surprised you haven't caught the eye of some preacher by now."

Whoa, hold up, Kara thought. Was that *shade*? Was little Miss Minnie Mouse trying to rub Kara's single status in her face?

"Actually, I'm dating Zachary," Kara said, gesturing toward their praise and worship team leader and once again lying within the house of the Lord. "We're real low-key with our relationship though. Honestly, I haven't really dated since Matthew and I broke up." She then leaned in toward Madison. "I've been celibate for years. But I'm sure you can relate." Kara was willing to bet Madison was a virgin when she met Matthew. She wanted to make sure Madison was aware that she had Matthew first in more ways than one.

Before Madison could reply, Matthew joined them. "What are you two over here whispering about?"

"Kara was just telling me about her boyfriend, the praise and worship team leader," Madison replied.

Kara tried to hide a smirk. It seemed Madison couldn't wait to let it be known that Kara was taken, making it clear to Matthew that she was off limits. Kara searched Matthew's face for any sign of jealousy but his expression remained neutral.

"Oh really? That's awesome. He's a very gifted worship leader. Matter of fact, we're in search of another worship team leader. You think he can recommend anyone?"

"I'll ask him for you," Kara said. She didn't want to risk Matthew approaching him and her lie about them dating being exposed. It wouldn't be too hard to convince Zachary to play along though. He'd been flirting with her since coming to Holy Ground over two years ago. Kara knew he'd be tickled about the ruse.

****

But it was a ruse that took on a life of its own because a couple of weeks after the church anniversary both Kara and Zachary ended up joining Matthew's church, Faith Temple.

Bishop Steepleton had confronted his daughter about her theatrics, telling her he didn't appreciate her using the church's platform to showboat in front of Matthew. Feeling like a chastened child, Kara went to visit Matthew's church the following Sunday in retaliation. She'd enjoyed the service so much that by the time she left that afternoon, she'd decided to become a member. But Kara knew she had to play it cool and visit more on the sly before joining. She even went so far as convincing Zachary to talk to Matthew about his vacant worship team leader position. Zachary was more than happy to do so. Faith Temple's praise team often participated in highly publicized gospel concerts. Zachary felt this would increase his chances of being discovered by a music executive and signing a lucrative recording contract. Matthew told Zachary that he would be glad to have him on board, but it was important for him to discuss things over with Bishop Steepleton first. He prided himself as a man of integrity and didn't feel comfortable with just 'stealing' Zachary away from Holy Ground. The Bishop was disappointed with Zachary's departure but told Matthew he appreciated him reaching out to him first. When it came to Kara, Bishop Steepleton said that his daughter was wise enough to make her own decisions and if switching church homes is what she wanted, then he wasn't at liberty to try and stop her.

Kara reasoned that she'd desired to seek out a new church home for quite some time. Playing the role of the good Bishop's daughter at Holy Ground had gotten old and she was ready for a change. Her father was old school and she liked Matthew's more relatable style of preaching. Faith Temple was more hip and in touch with the new church trends.

Kara did her best to make a good impression with Madison. She wanted her secret nemesis to have no inkling that she was still in love with Matthew, which is why she and Zachary kept up the charade of being a couple. Kara convinced him that their dating ploy would benefit them both. He had a better shot at securing a music deal and she'd get her man back. But of course, gossip soon flew around Faith Temple and it didn't take long for word to spread that she was Matthew's ex-girlfriend. Kara had the misfortune of overhearing a couple of female members discussing her in the restroom after service one Sunday.

"Chile, she ain't fooling nobody. I bet she wants to get back with Pastor. We gotta keep our eyes on her. First Lady is too trusting and naïve. But I know this Kara chick's kind. All of them preachers' daughters think they entitled to take all the good pastors.

"I hear you, Cyndra. You remember how hard she was putting on for Pastor Harding at that anniversary? Looking like Phaedra Parks. Just a hot mess."

Everything within Kara wanted to make her presence known and set it off with these holy hussies but she stayed quiet, remained in the stall, and waited for them to leave the restroom. But they were on her radar and she vowed to make them regret their words one day when she became Matthew's new wife. Her main order of business was getting Matthew to realize he'd made a mistake in marrying Madison. And it was almost like divine intervention when Zachary called her one evening with a bombshell.

"Whoa…say that again?" Kara asked, not believing what she was hearing.

"First Lady Madison starred in an adult video," Zachary revealed.

"Zachary, stop playing."

"I kid you not, Kare Bear." He laughed. Kara hated when he called her that.

"Who told you this?"

"I saw it with my own eyes. I was up late one night surfing the web and - "

"Wait…never mind. I get it," Kara said, hiding her disgust. "But are you sure it was her? It could be someone who resembles her."

"You want me to send you the link to the video?" Zachary asked.

Kara was all set to decline but she realized if she were to go to Matthew with this information she had to be sure. So she told Zachary to send it. Kara felt filthy watching the video but, it was indeed First Lady Madison. A much younger Madison, but still her nonetheless. Kara figured the video was made when she was in her early twenties. Kara wondered if Matthew was aware of his wife's past.

She began to map out just how she would reveal to him and the church that he had wed a former porno star. But first she wanted to have some fun toying with Madison about her secret past.

"You were born and raised in Alabama, correct?" Kara asked Madison one day during their monthly church brunch. "You ever thought about doing any acting?"

Madison chuckled. "The closest I've come to Hollywood was when I briefly attended UCLA."

Bingo! That explained how Madison even got mixed up in the shady film industry. Kara highly doubted the video was done in Huntsville, Alabama. It had California love written all over it.

"Wow, I can imagine that California was quite a cultural shock after coming from a small town," Kara said.

They continued to make conversation and Kara learned that Madison had dropped out of college to take care of her ailing father. But Kara suspected her exodus from California had more to do with her trying to leave her past life behind. Kara decided to hire a private investigator to get more dirt on Mrs. Madison Harding. It upset Kara that women like her were still single while the Madisons of the world snatched up all of the decent men. There was no reason for a beautiful woman like Kara to be single while this Jezebel-in-disguise had *her* man. Madison was nothing but a fraud and Kara despised hypocritical Christians.

She also couldn't wait to stop this façade with Zachary because he was just as repulsive. Getting up each Sunday to lead praise and worship while moonlighting with the devil and watching nasty videos. She hoped that demonic spirit of lust within him didn't transfer throughout the atmosphere as he sang. But Kara reasoned that the Bible spoke of how all things worked together for good. Zachary's lust of the flesh would be the catalyst to rid Madison from Matthew's life. Kara was sure this was God propelling her toward her rightful place as Matthew's next wife.

The private investigator uncovered that Madison also worked as an escort while at UCLA. Kara couldn't sit on all this information any longer and was ready to expose Madison before the church, conspiring with Zachary to play the video via the church monitors. He was initially reluctant but changed his mind once Kara added a cash incentive to the deal. She considered it an investment into her future.

Kara bounced into church that particular Sunday, ready to set her plan into motion. Madison was in her usual position right outside of the main sanctuary, greeting the members as they entered. But Kara's mouth dropped open as her eyes landed on a woman standing next to Madison. She wore a form fitting hot pink jumpsuit, looking as if she was about to take the stage at a strip club rather than enter a church. But what was even more shocking was that the woman looked exactly like Madison.

Spotting Kara, Madison smiled and waved her over. "Good morning, Kara. I'd like to introduce you to my identical twin sister, Michelle."

Kara just gaped. But this Michelle didn't even acknowledge Kara's presence anyhow. Turning to her sister and sucking her teeth she asked if service was about to start soon. "You know I don't like being up in church all day."

"Yes, we're about to start in five minutes. Kara, you'll have to excuse my sister. She can be such a heathen." Madison laughed. "Michelle, why don't you go inside and find a seat?"

Without another word Michelle went into the sanctuary, giving the male members an eyeful of her ample backside as she strode down the aisle.

Taking in Kara's stunned expression, Madison laughed. "The fact that I'm a twin surprises most people. Michelle and I were separated when our parents divorced. She grew up in California with our mom while I remained in Alabama with our father. I've always been a Daddy's girl." Madison explained. When Kara didn't say anything Madison peered at her closely.

"Hey, Kara, are you okay? You look as if you're about to be sick."

Finally gathering her bearings, Kara managed to nod. "Y-yes, I'm fine. Just a little hot. You know how this Houston heat is. I worked up a sweat just walking from my car into the church. I'm going to head into the ladies room to freshen up a bit before service." Kara could only imagine how lame she sounded but she couldn't get away from Madison fast enough.

Once inside of the ladies room she leaned against a sink, dumbfounded. Her heart felt like it had sunk into her stomach. Why hadn't that stupid investigator told her about the twin sister? The person in the video was obviously Michelle. She couldn't believe she'd come so close to making a total fool of herself in front of the congregation with her outlandish claims against Madison.

Her emotions were churning and she decided there was no way she could sit through service. Kara had just exited the church, headed towards her car when she heard Madison call her name.

"What's wrong, Kara? You look like you've lost your best friend. Or maybe you're upset because you finally understand that you've lost your man." Madison said, giving Kara the most contemptuous stare. "You were really going to put me out on front street today, huh?"

Kara frowned in confusion. "What do you mean?"

"You know exactly what I mean!" Madison hissed. "Zachary told me all about your plan. He's been flirting with me since coming here. Then had the nerve to try and extort money out of me for his silence about the video. I knew he wasn't one to be trusted when he just up and left your father's church like he did."

Kara couldn't believe Zachary had double-crossed her. "B-but we were wrong. It was obviously your twin sister."

"Oh no, it was *me* on that video. You think y'all are the first to try and expose me? Matthew believes it's Michelle on the video as well. There's nothing my sister wouldn't do for me. She gave me the opportunity to turn my life around after my seedy past. And I won't let a desperate and pathetic woman like you ruin my new life. You're lucky I'm a woman of God now, otherwise I'd call Michelle out here and we'd kick your thirsty behind all over this parking lot." Madison said, laughing as she saw the fear in Kara's eyes.

"Don't worry. I'm not gonna hurt you. But if you know what's good for you, make this your last Sunday at Faith Temple. And take that pervert Zachary with you. If you don't leave, I'll tell Matthew how treacherous the both of you are. Lying about being a couple and betraying your own father to come over here and sniff behind my man. Now take your tail home and write Matthew a nice letter stating that you're returning to Holy Ground. And this time try to actually get some of that *holiness* down in you."

With those last words, Madison turned on her heels and sashayed back into the church. Kara was at a total loss for words. As she got into her car she realized she'd greatly underestimated First Lady Madison Harding. It was amazing how the best laid plans had a tendency to backfire. Kara was certain by the time she left church that afternoon she'd have gotten rid of Madison. Instead, Madison had gotten rid of her. But what hurt the most was the hard truth that any chance of getting Matthew back was gone forever. It was a truth as bitter as the tears of shame and humiliation that coursed down her cheeks.

Starting her car, Kara decided to heed Madison's advice. If she hurried she could make it to Holy Ground in time to catch her father's sermon. The prodigal daughter was returning home.

The End

Sherron Elise *is a proud native of Houston, Texas. An avid reader since childhood, her passion for getting lost within the pages of a book soon transformed into using her vivid imagination to create stories of her own. You can find out more info about Sherron and her books at www.sherronelise.com.*

6

I WANT THAT OLD THANG BACK

By Corey Bu-Shea

"I want her back, man," I lamented to my best friend, Marcus. We were rookies with the Greensboro Wolfers. Both signed to three-year contracts, although mine had a few more million, since I was the main shooting guard, but we had been best friends since kindergarten. Two rough-and-tumble boys, being raised by single mothers, who shared a love of basketball. We had seen it all, been through it all, and well, here we were.

"Bruh, Keisha does not want your ass back, not after she caught you with those twins. What were their names? Candy and Mandy?" Marcus said as he plopped down on the expensive, black leather sectional, which covered at least three-fourths of my living room.

"Don't remind me. It was my bachelor party. I was just trying to have just one more night of fun, before I took the plunge."

"Well, I don't think Keisha thought you would be plunging in another woman's pool. Oh, let me correct myself, two women's pools." Marcus laughed like this was really funny.

"All right, man, knock it off," I told him as I took a seat in the matching black leather recliner across from him.

"I am just sayin'. All of that sticking and moving that you have been doing. All of the TMZ and Bossip stories. You had to know that she was going to get fed up one day."

"Yeah, I guess you right. But I didn't expect her not to take my calls, or not answer the door when I went to her apartment."

"What did you expect? For the two of you to be BFF's after you cheated on her not once, but throughout your relationship, and then to finally catch you in the act?"

I shook my head. "Speaking of which, I still can't figure out how she found out about the hotel, the twins…did she have GPS tracking device or a PI following me?"

"You know that women's intuition is a motherfucker, man. Which is why I stay single, for shizzle."

"Your crusty ass stay single, because despite your million dollar basketball salary, you are a scrub."

He shot me the finger and went back to messing with his phone. Usually, I liked talking shit with my boy, but today, it wasn't making me feel any better. Marcus made a lot of sense, which he always did, but I wanted my girl back. Keisha and I had been together since freshman year of high school. I just knew that she and I would be the next Lebron and Savannah or Kobe and Vanessa, but I had fucked up one time too many.

"Yo man, I'll be back." I jumped up. Grabbed my coat off the couch, and headed toward the door. I hit the key fob on my cobalt blue Benz, and immediately turned on Pandora to the Monica channel, who was Keisha's favorite artist. Usually, driving around helped me clear my mind. I had been doing that quite a bit since Keisha and I had broken up four months earlier, but today I had a specific destination and purpose in mind.

I arrived at Friendly Shopping Center, Greensboro's largest mall, which was really just a slew of shops with various buildings for the super-rich, and the ones who thought they were. Since Keisha was deadset on avoiding me, I thought I would meet her on her territory. Keisha was a diehard fan and shopper of Bath and Body Works, and I knew they were having a 50% off sale today, which she loved. If I had to wait in the store all day, there was no way that I was going to miss an opportunity to speak to my baby. Four months was enough time for someone to cool off, right? Well, it had to be. I had tried giving her space, but I needed her in my life. I had never considered monogamy. Hell, I was a twenty-seven-year-old pro-athlete. Expecting me to be monogamous was like putting a fat kid in front of a stack of freshly baked cookies and daring them to touch them. It was damn near impossible. But there was this huge void in my life without Keisha, so if she told me to walk barefoot on a bed of nails, I was willing to do it.

I entered the store and went into straight PI/Macgyver mode, peering over the crowd of shoppers to see if I could catch a glimpse of her. I had no idea what I was going to say. I was going to just speak from my heart, and hope that hers still had a soft spot for me.

"May I help you sir?" said the redhead salesclerk, with the too-perky voice and fake smile. She really wasn't trying to help me; what she really meant was, 'what is your kind doing in this store in the super rich Friendly Avenue area of Greensboro?' It was the look every white person gave people of color on this side of town.

"Nah, I'm good," I said, trying to remain unthreatening, while keeping my hands firmly in my pocket. You couldn't make sudden moves as a big black man around white folks; it made them too nervous.

"Oh my, God. Are you Tarik Owens?" a woman asked me. "My dad is the biggest fan of yours. Can we take a selfie?"

Before I could even respond, the woman who looked like she could be twins with Miranda from "Sex in the City" had whipped out her iPhone.

Not wanting to appear a complete jackass, I acquiesced.

"Sure." I allowed her to invade my personal space by stepping right beside me and clicking a quick pic.

"My dad is not going to believe this. I met THE Tarik Owens. Thank you so much!"

"You're welcome." I tried to be gracious as possible to my fans, but I really wanted her away from me. I was here for one purpose, and that was to reclaim the love of my life. It wouldn't be a good look if Keisha saw me with another woman.

I wandered around aimlessly in the store for another five minutes, pretending to look at the merchandise, while hoping no one else recognized me.

I heard the door chime, and as I'd been doing every time I heard that sound, I turned my head toward the front. And there she was. Looking like a pure vision. Dressed modestly in a pair of True Religion jeans and a charcoal gray hooded sweatshirt.

We locked eyes and I could see she was surprised. She quickly averted her eyes to the ground as if to avoid me. But we were going to have this conversation. We meant too much to each other to just leave things unsettled. If she didn't want to see me or be a part of my life, she was going to have to tell me to my face.

I walked over to her. "You look well."

"Really, Tarik? We haven't seen each other in four months, and the first thing you do is compliment me on my looks?"

"What was I supposed to say, Keisha? You won't take any of my calls; you won't even answer the door when I drop by your apartment. After four months of you ghosting me, I guess I decided small talk was the way to start."

"Tarik, There's nothing to talk about. There is nothing left to say. I've moved on, and you should try to do the same."

"What's that supposed to mean? You've moved on? Are you telling me you got another nigga already?" I was starting to get heated. It had only been four months. I mean yeah, I had gotten some ass here and there to keep the blue balls away, but I wasn't serious about anyone and she knew that.

"Tarik, everybody is not like you. No, I don't have another nigga, as you say. I am doing me. Means I am tired of your bullshit, and I am enjoying being single."

"Look, Keisha. I know that I have put you through a lot and if I said sorry a thousand times, it wouldn't be enough. But I am going to do better," I pleaded.

"How many times in the last thirteen years have I heard that I am sorry, and that you are going to do better? You haven't been faithful to me a day in your life since I met you when I was fourteen. At twenty-seven, I deserve better, and I will not be my mom, or any of those other NBA wives."

"What can I do to make it right? What can I do to get another chance? Do you want me to beg? Do you want a bigger ring? Do you want me to pledge monogamy? Whatever you want, I will give it to you." I could only imagine what I looked like begging this woman over a display of Eucalyptus Stress Relief candles.

"I want to move on, Tarik. I want you to realize that we are done. I want you to promise that you will treat your next woman better. That is what I want from you." Her eyes watered.

"Come on, Keisha. Don't the past thirteen years mean anything to you?"

She stared at me in disbelief. "Are you actually listening to yourself right now? Your dumb ass is standing here acting like I am the one who wronged you, like I cheated. Like I am the one who had groupies. Like I am the one who exposed you to all types of STD's and tabloid fodder." Her tears had suddenly become angry tears.

"I know but -"

She held up a finger to cut me off. "Nah, you don't know, but you are about to find out. I am tired, Tarik, and now I have more than me to think about."

"What?" I knew women sometimes spoke in riddles, but what was she talking about?

I got my answer pretty quickly as Keisha pulled up the bottom half of her hoodie, and revealed a slight baby bump.

What? I was going to be a daddy! The overwhelming elation I felt right now was indescribable. I was about to have my first child with a woman who I was madly in love with, not some groupie; she had to give us another chance.

"Are you telling me what I think you are, Keisha?"

"Yes, Tarik. I'm pregnant. I am about four months."

"This changes everything, baby. I am not going to be a part-time dad, and you're not going to be a single mother. We can finally get married, start over. Like I said before, I will give you anything you want. I just want you and my child to be okay."

"It's not yours." Keisha dropped her head and averted my eyes.

Had I heard what I thought I heard? Did the woman who I have loved for the last thirteen years of my life, just tell me the baby she was carrying wasn't mine?

"Stop trippin', Keisha. I know you're mad, but you don't have to play games like this. This is a whole other level of petty, even for you."

"I'm not playing any games. The baby is really not yours."

"What the fuck you mean the baby isn't mine? Who the fuck's is it?"

"It's mine." I heard a familiar voice right behind me. *No, this couldn't be, not him.*

I turned around in the direction of that voice; there stood my best friend of over twenty years, Marcus. He had this big, shit-eating grin on his face, like he had just won the NBA championship and not torn my heart into a million pieces and turned my world upside down. I moved toward him with my fists clinched; I was having the worst day of my life, and his was about to get ten times worse!

"Stop it, Tarik. You will not make a scene, around these white people," Keisha said through clinched teeth, as she firmly grabbed my balled-up fist.

"Why you do it, man? Why did you sleep with my girl?" I was bordering on being fighting mad, as my eyes narrowed in slits, but I also felt like crying, and I could feel the water collecting in my tear ducts. I wasn't about to let either one of them see me cry though; I wasn't about to give them that satisfaction.

He smirked and shrugged nonchalantly. "Man, you've always had the bigger athletic talent, the bigger contract, always got the girl. When Keisha came to me for comfort after finding you with the twins the night before your wedding, I guess I saw my opportunity to even the score a little."

I was floored. "You did this because you were jealous of me? What kind of shit is that?"

Keisha still had her grip on my arm and customers were starting to stare. Two NBA players fighting in the middle of Bath and Body Works would be all she wrote for TMZ, Bossip, and MediaTakeout. There would be team suspensions, endorsement deals pulled. That thought made me pause.

No. I wasn't going to be the next Ron Artest or Dennis Rodman; my grandmother had raised me better than that.

I jerked my arm from Keisha's grasp; shot both a death stare, that would have murdered both of them on the spot, if stares alone could kill, and just exited the same door that I had entered a little less than an hour before.

My grandmother once told me as one of her many life lessons, "If you watch your closest friend, your enemy will never do you any harm."

I had my eye on my enemy, and now I had lost my two best friends!

The End

Corey Bu-Shea is the author of two previous nonfiction works: Let Not Your Heart Be Troubled, and I Have Some Shit to Say. Bu-Shea is a college instructor, who loves social media, and can be reached on Twitter @coreybking or Facebook corey.bushea.

7

PERFECT TIMING

By Tamika Lucas

Another night alone, Danielle thought as she tossed the empty container of butter pecan gelato in the trash. She'd only planned to eat a few spoonfuls. But one scoop led to another, now the entire gallon was gone. The regret was immediate.

Danielle settled on the living room sofa in her plush bathrobe and foam hair rollers. Her gaze traveled from the television to the front door awaiting her husband, Richard's arrival.

Danielle remembered when Richard gave her the courtesy of telling her he'd be working late. Nowadays, he just showed up before sunrise.

I have to work when there's work because there may not always be work. Danielle recalled one of Richard's quips as a homebuilder. She didn't know contractors worked until midnight. But that was Richard. He was a workaholic.

The two of them were high school sweethearts. When they got married nineteen years ago, their connection was so deeply intense it was like God himself had arranged it. Lately, the only time they talked was about their eighteen-year-old son, Joshua. And Danielle couldn't remember the last time Richard touched her. He barely even looked at her.

Danielle's eyelids were heavy. She glanced at the clock on the wall. It was 10:59 p.m., just in time for the Powerball drawing. Danielle rarely played the lottery. But today, when she strolled into the convenience store to replenish her supply of Flamin' Hot Cheetos, she had a hunch to purchase a lottery ticket.

Glancing at her ticket, she studied the numbers before she looked at the screen. *3-13-20-32-33-21*. Danielle's heartbeat accelerated as she stared at the winning Powerball numbers on the television. She looked closer at her lottery ticket, then grabbed the remote control, rewound and replayed the numbers.

A perfect match.

Danielle's lips stretched into a smile that reached her eyes.

"Two hundred and forty-seven million dollars! We're rich! Rich! Thank you, Jesus!"

Danielle leaped. She waved her hands in the air and broke out into the cabbage patch, her signature dance move.

She couldn't wait to tell Richard they were multi-millionaires and their lives were about to change forever.

Danielle heard the keys rattling at the door. *There he is.* She smiled even wider when Richard walked through the door. No matter what time of the day, the sight of her husband put a smile on Danielle's face. He was just that fine. When he wasn't working, he was at the gym. He had the body to prove it. At forty, he was in better shape than most men in their twenties.

Richard entered the house with his cell phone to his ear. He was so engrossed in conversation he didn't notice Danielle dancing around the living room. He wore a stiffly starched white button down and khaki pants. Danielle often wondered why Richard's clothes looked and smelled freshly laundered on his workdays.

"I'm going to do it tonight. I promise," Richard said before hanging up the phone.

Danielle leaped into Richard's arms.

"Richard, you're not going to believe this. I...."

"Danielle, sit down. We need to talk."

Richard's tone was stern and solemn. Danielle knew it was serious.

Danielle sat down on the living room sofa where she'd just received the best news of her life. She had a feeling what Richard had to say wasn't good at all.

"I want a divorce."

Danielle felt herself getting lightheaded. Did she just hear correctly?

Divorce.

"I have a confession to make. I'm in love with someone else. We're getting married. We have two children. Chloe is two and Richard Jr. is three."

Danielle couldn't move. She couldn't even speak. All she could do was think how good the ceramic vase on the mantel would look shattered on top of Richard's head.

"I would have left a long time ago, but I wanted to wait until Joshua turned eighteen. I want all my kids to be raised in a two-parent household. Now that I'm done raising Joshua, I need to raise my other children. And since Joshua's starting college in a few months, I figured now is the perfect time."

Richard paced the living room. "I haven't been happy in years. Things haven't been the same between us. You gained weight and we just don't have fun like we used to."

I know this fool ain't divorcing me because I gained thirty pounds.

"Danielle." He stared at her when she didn't respond. "Danielle? Danielle, please say something."

Danielle still couldn't speak. She was heartbroken and furious. But with one thought of her lottery winnings, euphoria consumed her again. She did something even she didn't expect. She burst into laughter.

"Do you need help packing?"

Danielle didn't give him time to answer as she hastened to their master bedroom closet. She threw Richard's clothes in suitcases, not even bothering to remove the hangers.

"Whew! You have a lot of clothes. You're gonna need boxes. Do we have boxes in the garage?"

"I th-think so," Richard stammered.

"Let me check," Danielle said.

Danielle went to the garage and came back with two large boxes.

Richard knitted his eyebrows together.

"You're taking this a lot better than I thought."

"Like you said, the timing could not have been more perfect."

Danielle emptied Richard's socks and underwear into one of the boxes. There was just enough room for his neckties.

"I don't have to leave this moment."

Danielle cackled. "Yeah. Actually you do. Your fiancé and kids are waiting for you, remember? What's your address? I'll just call a moving company to pack up your things and deliver them tomorrow."

Danielle grabbed a pencil and pad from the nightstand.

"Um...uh....it's 6765 Fairfield Lane, Houston, Texas 77022," Richard said.

Danielle paused. That was Tanya Leonard's address. Tanya was Richard's twenty-five-year-old administrative assistant. He built her house last year. She distinctively remembered the luxury upgrades that weren't in any of Richard's custom homes. It was the best-looking house he'd ever built. Danielle's hurt grew deeper. Their home needed major repairs and Danielle could hardly get Richard to change a light bulb.

"So, you're leaving me for Tanya Leonard?"

Richard nodded.

"Wow! This just keeps getting better and better."

"What is that supposed to mean?"

"Oh, nothing."

Tanya was pretty. Danielle would give her that. But that was all. Danielle and Tanya's sister, Tiffany, frequented the same hair salon. She'd heard all about Tanya's romantic trysts with married men. Richard was just one of several married men she was seeing.

"When are you going to tell Joshua?" Danielle placed Richard's sneakers in the second box.

"I was hoping you would take care of that," Richard said, fidgeting.

"No. I think you should since this is your idea. I'm sure he'll be surprised to hear he has a baby brother and a baby sister." Danielle handed Richard the box containing his sneakers. "Have you spoken with an attorney?"

"Not yet."

"Let's not wait a minute longer," she replied. "I'll contact mine first thing in the morning,"

"I agree." He looked around the bedroom. "You can keep the house. But I'm not paying alimony."

"Richard, I don't need or want a dime of your money," Danielle snapped.

Danielle hadn't worked in the nineteen years she and Richard had been married. She had dreams of becoming an interior designer, but Richard talked her into being a stay-at-home mom. It was a decision she always regretted.

Danielle rolled the last piece of Richard's luggage to the front door.

"Okay. That's it. I'll have the rest of your stuff delivered to you tomorrow. And my attorney will be in touch."

Richard smiled. "I can't believe you're cool about this. I've been dreading this day for years. But you've made all of this so easy for me. Thank you."

When Danielle heard Richard's ignition, she fell to the floor and sobbed. She'd just won the lottery, but she felt like she'd just lost everything.

****

"So, let me get this straight. You won the Powerball, but you want to give me your ticket?" Danielle's sister, Rhonda, repeated for the third time. Rhonda was two years Danielle's senior. Danielle called her over for breakfast to share the news of her lottery win and impending divorce.

"Yes."

"First of all, I don't believe you. Second, if you actually won the Powerball, why on earth would you give your ticket away?"

Danielle handed Rhonda the lottery ticket and pointed to the winning numbers on the lottery commission's website on her cell phone.

"See. Now, do you believe me?"

Rhonda gripped Danielle's arm.

"Oh my gosh! Oh my gosh! I can't believe this! Sis, you're rich!"

"That's what I've been trying to tell you the whole time," Danielle said, taking a bite of her blueberry pancakes.

"That explains why Richard's clothes are all over the sofa. You guys must be moving."

"No. That's the other news. Richard and I are getting a divorce. The movers are coming shortly to get the rest of his belongings."

Rhonda gasped. "Oh no. I'm sorry, sis. What happened?"

"Last night, when I was getting ready to tell him I won the Powerball, he told me he wanted a divorce."

She frowned. "But why?"

"He said he's not happy, that I gained too much weight and he's in love with Tanya Leonard. They're getting married."

"Tanya Leonard? The Tanya Leonard with the waist-long weave, five-inch eyelashes and the surgically enhanced body?"

"That's her."

Rhonda's mouth gaped open.

"They have two kids together. He said he wanted to be a present father for their children since he is done raising Joshua. Hell, I'm the one who raised Joshua."

"But doesn't she have like five kids."

"I don't know. I lost count."

"Wow! I'm speechless. You better get tested. Everyone, and I mean everyone, knows Tanya Leonard. I thought Richard was one of the good guys."

"The sad part is, I didn't even know he was unhappy. All those late nights he claimed to be working, he was really with her. I feel like such a fool." Danielle shook her head.

"So, since I must report all my marital assets during the divorce proceedings, Richard cannot find out I won the Powerball. I refuse to split my fortune with him, so he can spend it all on Tanya. That's why I want to give you the ticket. I would rather share my fortune with you."

Rhonda's eyes welled up with water. "Come on. Don't play with me."

"I'm serious."

Rhonda wrapped her arms around Danielle, squeezing her tightly. "Wow! Just wow! I don't know what to say."

"Just say you'll do it."

"Yes! Of course, I will."

"I've been doing my research. You have 180 days to claim the winnings. If you want to remain anonymous, you can set up a blind trust. Once my divorce is final, you can give me my half of the money. That way Richard won't be able to touch it."

"Sounds like you've really thought about this. Richard has no idea what he just walked out on.

Danielle stuffed her mouth with bacon. "Do you know a good divorce lawyer."

Rhonda nodded. "Do you remember Donovan Woods?"

Donovan had a crush on Danielle in high school. He was a nice but a little too skinny for Danielle's taste.

"I remember him," Danielle said.

"He's one of the best lawyers in Houston. I saw him the other day in Whole Foods. He asked about you. He's single and he's not scrawny like he used to be."

"Please, give me his number," Danielle said. Maybe a no-longer scrawny man was exactly what she needed to not only help her end her divorce, but get over it, too.

****

It had only been three months since Richard married Tanya and he was already having regrets. Tanya was never home. Richard was raising all five of their children alone, three of which weren't biologically his. Tanya didn't cook or clean, things Richard believed a wife should do. The only thing she did consistently was spend his money.

Tanya maxed out two of Richard's credit cards and stole money from his business account. Two of Richard's employees quit because he couldn't make payroll. He'd had to take on a second job as an electrician just to pay the bills.

Richard cleared the kitchen table. While loading the dishwasher, he noticed the walls and floor were splattered with remnants of his spaghetti dinner. Richard sighed. *These kids always make a mess.* Richard knew he would be up late again, cleaning up.

Richard glanced at the clock. "Taye, Aiden, Sydney, RJ and Chloe, it's time for bed."

Chloe yawned and reached for Richard. "Daddy, will you please read me a bedtime story?"

"Sure, honey." Richard lifted Chloe in his arms. He grabbed Chloe's favorite book, *Good Night Moon* from the bookshelf. Tanya approached him from behind. She had on a black mini skirt and fitted tank top, the same mini skirt that made Richard forget his wedding vows to Danielle.

"Where are you going?"

"To the hair salon."

Richard looked Tanya over. Her hair looked just fine to him.

"At nine at night?"

"Yeah. What's wrong with that?"

"I didn't know hair stylists take clients this late."

"My stylist does."

"Why did you shower and put on makeup just to get your hair done?"

"Would you prefer if I went stinky? Please stop with the questions. I never questioned you when you went home to Danielle every night," Tanya countered.

"I just know you keep going out late and getting home after midnight," he replied. "I left my wife, so we could be together but now it's like you don't even want me anymore. Are you cheating on me?"

"Of course not. I married you, didn't I? You're just going to have to trust me." She adjusted her skirt, then looked around the room. "Now, where's your wallet?"

"It's on the nightstand," Richard mumbled.

"Thanks, honey. I love you."

Tanya kissed Chloe on the cheek when she returned from the bedroom. "Please put the kids to sleep. It'll be late when I return."

Tanya blew Richard a kiss and headed out the front door.

****

Danielle whipped her brand new 2020 Range Rover into the driveway. She'd always wanted a Range Rover, now she owned two. After sharing her lottery winnings with Rhonda, Danielle had over 100 million dollars left. That was more than enough for her to live a lush life.

Danielle had just returned from a two-week trip to Dubai with Rhonda. In the last few months they'd traveled to Paris, St. Lucia and the Maldives. They stayed at five-star luxury resorts, shopped at high end boutiques and ate at the finest restaurants just because they could.

Danielle had become a new woman. She'd lost over fifty pounds (with the help of the best trainer in Houston), gotten a makeover, purchased a closet full of the latest designer fashions and just signed a purchase contract on a 20,000 square foot luxury estate in the most exclusive subdivision in Houston.

Danielle placed 20 million dollars in a trust fund for Joshua, paid for his college education and surprised him with a Tesla Model S for his birthday. Although she wanted to tell Joshua she won the lottery, she didn't want him accidentally blurting the news to Richard. So, she told him the car and the money were courtesy of his Aunt Rhonda's lottery winnings.

Danielle glanced at the For-Sale sign in front of the house she'd called home for the past nineteen years. There were so many fond memories of Joshua and happier times with Richard in the house. Every room, every corner had a story. The For-Sale sign made it real. That chapter of her life was over for good.

Danielle looked around the house to make sure everything was in place. Her neighbor, Sue, had been housesitting and watering her plants while she was on vacation. There wasn't much there. Danielle donated most of her furniture to Goodwill. All that remained was the guest bedroom furniture, the kitchen table set, a flat screen television and a chaise lounge in the living room.

Danielle showered and threw on a Victoria Secret's lounge set. She pulled her shoulder length hair in a ponytail, rolled on her MAC lip gloss, and slid on her memory foam slippers. She flopped onto the chaise lounge and grabbed the remote control.

Donovan was coming over with dinner in an hour. Ever since Donovan represented Danielle during her divorce, they'd been spending a lot of time together. Donovan wasn't the skinny teenager Danielle knew in high school. He was well-toned, charming, and stunningly handsome. And while she was nowhere near ready for a serious relationship, she enjoyed his company.

The doorbell rang. Donovan was a half hour early, Danielle thought as she hurried to the door. Her heart sank when she saw Richard standing in the threshold with a bouquet of roses.

"Richard? What are you doing here?"

"Hello, Danielle. These are for you."

Danielle reluctantly took the roses. Richard smiled and that was about the only thing that looked familiar. He looked like a completely different man. His hair was unkempt, he needed a shave, his clothes were dingy and wrinkled.

"May I please come in?"

Danielle shrugged as she stepped aside.

"Wow. You lost weight. You look amazing." Richard examined Danielle from head to toe. "Are you selling the house?" he continued when she didn't answer.

Danielle nodded.

"Why? This is our home. We have so many memories here." Richard surveyed the house.

"This *used* to be our home. Now, it's just a house."

"I saw two Range Rovers in the driveway. Do you have company?"

"No. They're mine."

Richard snickered. "You're joking, right?"

"No. I paid cash for both of them."

Richard knitted his brows. "You must've gotten a really good job."

Danielle took deep breaths. She pursed her lips to keep from telling Richard she'd won the Powerball just moments before he announced he wanted a divorce. Instead, she tried to be nonchalant. "Rhonda won the Powerball. She gave me over $100 million dollars."

Richard's eyes grew wide. "Rhonda won the Powerball? What are the odds?"

"One in 247 million," Danielle mumbled with a smirk.

"So, you're a millionaire?"

"A multi-millionaire. And had you not cheated on me with Tanya, you'd be a multi-millionaire, too." Okay, so she couldn't resist. She had to gloat a little.

Richard put his hand on his forehead. "Dang, I really, really messed up."

Danielle glared at Richard. "Why are you here?"

He sighed and looked her in the eyes. "Danielle, I made a big mistake. I miss you. I must've been going through some mid-life crisis when I got with Tanya. She cheated on me. I'm not even sure Chloe is mine. She ruined my life. She destroyed my business, my credit and took all my money. Everything I own is in the back of that U-Haul truck."

Danielle peered through the window. There was a 26-foot U-Haul truck in the driveway.

"I love you. I want to come back home. Is there anything I can do to fix this?" he pleaded.

Danielle knew this day would come, but she didn't think Richard would be begging to come back home so soon.

Danielle walked closer to Richard. "So, you want to divorce the wife you left your other wife for, in order to be with the wife you had all along?"

"Yeah. S-something like that," Richard stuttered.

Danielle could see the hurt in Richard's eyes. She almost felt sorry for him.

"Because things didn't work out with Tanya, you think you can just come back to me? Do you really think I'm that desperate?" she asked.

"No. But I know what we had was special. It was real. And I know you still love me," Richard said.

"There may be a part of me that will always love you. But I will never forget how much you hurt me. You dropped me like yesterday's trash the second a younger woman started paying you some attention. I deserve better. So, no. It's over and there's no way in hell I'll ever take you back."

Richard blinked back tears and walked toward the front door.

Donovan appeared at the doorway with takeout from Nara Express, Danielle's favorite Thai restaurant. Danielle greeted him with a kiss on the cheek. Richard clenched his fists.

"Come on in. I'm starving."

Richard glowered at Donovan.

"Is this a bad time?"

Danielle smiled. "Not at all. Richard got lost on his way home. He was just leaving."

Danielle grinned as Richard walked to the U-Haul truck.

Four months ago, she couldn't imagine life without him, now she was glad to see him go.

Richard's divorce announcement was the best thing that happened to her. It couldn't have come at a better time. Danielle was free; free to enjoy her life, her newfound fortune and the companionship of a new man. And she couldn't be happier.

The End

Tamika Lucas *is the bestselling and award-winning co-author of* The Ex Chronicles Anthology *where her short story,* Her Sister's Boyfriend *is featured. Tamika has a passion for contemporary fiction and poetry. She is currently working on her debut novel. You can follow her on Instagram @tamikalucaswrites and twitter @tamikatlucas.*

8

LIE TO ME

By Michelle D. Rayford

"You know, Robyn is cheating on you, right?" Anthony says, adding sugar to his sweet tea as if he isn't ruining my life.

I pretend I don't hear him and concentrate on chewing the bite of smothered pork chops. Normally, I look forward to these monthly lunches with my brother and Mabel's Soul Food Shack does not disappoint. The place, with hard mismatched plastic seats and outdated rickety tables arranged haphazardly around the room is a shack tucked along the end of a strip mall outside of downtown Atlanta. We were lucky to score one of the only two booths with the cracked seats repaired with duct tape.

Robyn's cheating on you.

Wiping the sweat from my brow, I toss my tie over a

shoulder to avoid getting it messy from such awesome home-style cuisine. The lone ceiling fan is losing the battle between the heat from the kitchen and the bodies packed into a small space. I slice another piece of pork chop and savor the tender meat. Then I attack the macaroni and cheese with its blend of three cheeses swimming in enough butter to grease an entire six-foot adult. I scoop up a forkful and chance a glance at my brother.

"I know you heard me," Tony says.

He's right. Nothing wrong with my hearing. I put the fork down, knowing the butter beans will have to wait. "What are you talking about?"

Tony finishes stirring his drink and gulps half of the tea before he comes up for air. "You know, bro."

"Tell me what I know."

Tony pours more tea into his glass from the pitcher he insisted the waitress leave on our table. He starts the sugar ritual again, meaning he'll tell me in his own time. An annoying quirk that gets under my skin much like the burden of being the little brother of Anthony "Homerun" Harris.

Growing up, I thought my big brother was the coolest dude around. Popular athlete, star baseball player in high school and college. Me? I'm the opposite. Excelled at math, failed at being cool. Anthony always looked out for me, though. The problem is he is still doing it. Whether I want him to or not.

I take the reprieve and finish off my meal. No need to waste good homemade food. When I've cleaned the bone, impatience makes me ask, "Are you going to tell me what's up or not?"

Tony puts the empty glass on the table and burps. He leans back in the booth. "Here's the deal. You know how Monica's been bugging me about taking her to see the new Tyler Perry flick?"

"What? I mean, yeah, everybody knows your wife loves Tyler."

"She drives me crazy with that." Tony shakes his head. "Anytime the man releases a new movie or premieres a new show, I'm supposed to care. Perry got something new out every week and —"

"What does that have to do with Robyn?"

"I'm getting to it," he says, waving off my interruption. "So, I take my wife to see the flick. It was decent. At least the part I saw. I dozed off."

"Man, get to it," I say through my teeth.

Tony signals the weave-wearing waitress for more tea. He waits until the pitcher is full and continues. "I ask Monica if she wants to get something to eat. I suggest Miyabi's, you know the new hibachi restaurant next to the theater?"

He's killing me with the irrelevant parts of the story, but I nod anyway.

"We get taken to a table where there are already like three other couples. We order, and the guy's putting on a real good show."

"Man, if you don't get to the point——"

Tony holds up a hand and frowns. "Okay, okay. So, Monica gets up to go to the restroom and I turn to watch her walk away." He smiles showing all thirty-two teeth. "My baby still looks good."

Even through my frustration, I return that smile. My

brother has a great woman and a happy marriage. Same thing I'm hoping for.

"Anyway, who do I see at the table behind us but your girl, Robyn."

I let out a breath I didn't realize I was holding. "That's it? I knew she was going out with the ladies from the shop."

Tony sits up straight and dark brown eyes lock on mine. "She wasn't with no ladies. She was with a dude. It looked like they were on a date."

I shake my head. My Robyn on a date? No way.

Last night Robyn came in around midnight. Nothing unusual. Nights with the girls tend to run long. She was quiet when she tiptoed into the bedroom, went straight into the bathroom, and showered. When she crawled into bed, she turned her back to me and curled into her usual position. I spooned my body around her and kissed her neck, inhaling the familiar scent of her mango and peach body wash.

"You still awake?" she whispered.

I ground my pelvis into her ample behind. "Waiting on my baby."

She yawned and patted my arm. "I'm tired, Dre. I'll make it up to you tomorrow."

"Come on, baby." I pressed upon her my full length of need. "It's been a week."

"I know," she replied, yawning. "It's been really busy at the shop."

And you've been going out every night, I didn't add. I still wanted to get some. "Just a quickie. I need you, babe." I hated when she made me beg and it appears I was doing more of that lately.

"Yeah, like I need you to co-sign that line of credit," she mumbled.

"I promise I'll look at it first thing."

She didn't respond. I moved against her, but she let out an unlady-

like snore to shut me down.

The crash of dishes hitting the floor brings me back to the present. The chatter in the diner dips for a second, then resumes.

"Are you listening to me?" Tony asks.

I wipe my hands on a paper napkin and toss it on top of my plate. "I don't know what you thought you saw. Robyn went out with friends."

"That's your problem. You don't want to face the truth about things. You need to let go of the little fantasy you're wrapped up in."

"I've got to get back to the office." I reach for my wallet, but Tony stops me.

"It's my turn to pay. You got it last time."

I calculate the bill in my head and slide to the edge of the booth. Tony is a horrible tipper. "Make sure you leave at least five dollars for the tip."

"Hold up, Dre. Why you leaving like this? I'm looking out for fam, you know? I can't have my brother getting played."

I take a deep breath and stand. "I know, man. And I appreciate it. But me and Robyn are good."

Tony signals the waitress for the check. "You're a good dude. All romantic and shit. Some women will take advantage. She already got you investing in her business. Wasn't you supposed to take that money and expand your own accounting firm?"

"I was wondering how long it would take you to go there." I'm surprised he waited this long to work it into the conversation. He's never cared for Robyn.

"I'm just saying," he counters with a shrug. "Remember what happened with Lisa?"

You always remember the first woman who broke your heart.

"Robyn is nothing like Lisa." I made sure of it.

Tony throws up his hands. "All right, all right. Fine. But I know what I saw."

"And I know Robyn," I snap. "You're wrong."

I storm out of the place, yanking the car door open and collapsing into the leather seats. I do the breathing exercises the therapist recommended. When my fists unclench, I know it's safe to drive.

Leave it to Tony to ruin lunch at Mabel's. I don't care what he thought he saw. Robyn went out with friends last night. One of them brought a date. Yeah, that's what happened. I'm sure of it.

A patrol car appears in my rearview mirror and I check the speedometer. The last thing I need is another encounter with the police. I've been abiding by the restraining order Lisa had the audacity to file. I was only trying to have a conversation about what she did. I never had any plans to hurt her.

When their car passes me at the next intersection, I smile and activate the hands-free mode to reach my assistant. One of the perks of being the boss is that I can take the rest of the day off. My destination was established as soon as I left the diner.

Maybe it's time to spice things up in my relationship. Be more spontaneous. I pull into a parking space behind the beauty shop nestled in a more affluent area of Buckhead and imagine the surprise on Robyn's face when her man comes to take her to lunch.

I let myself in the back and enter Robyn's richly furnished office. I haven't been here since we moved the furniture in the small space six months ago. We painted the walls and hung a few pictures. I put together all the bookcases in the corner, and shelving that stretches the length of an entire wall. Took me an hour to move in the desk we picked out and position it just right. By the end of the day, I knew the smoke glass desk was a mistake. Much like the huge bouquet of flowers sitting on top of it. Flowers I didn't send.

Searching for a card, I reach into the vibrant display but come up empty. Three other women work here. I'm sure those flowers belong to one of them.

The door that leads to the salon is closed. I lean against it and listen for voices on the other side.

When I slowly open the door, the air is thick with steam and the scent of a fruity shampoo and chemicals invade my nostrils. Music plays from the local R&B station. The television mounted in the corner is on a cable news channel with the sound muted.

The women are engaged in some sort of debate and don't notice me at first. Robyn once told me that a beauty salon is worse than any barbershop talk. No subject is off limits.

"I'm just saying that there's no need to cheat. If you don't want to be with somebody, just let them go and move on," Naya says while braiding a lady's hair. Though her back is to me, her tall thin frame is rocking a pair of skinny jeans that highlight her tight ass.

"I don't know. Sometimes it's more complicated than that." This statement comes from Sonya who's at the shampoo bowl with a client. It's the most I've ever heard her speak. The short, bosomy woman with glossy hair rarely utters a word when I'm around.

"That's just being selfish," Naya responds. "What's so complicated about being greedy?"

Ms. Maxine, the oldest woman in the shop, runs a comb through her customer's silver colored hair. "Nothing as long as you know how to lie." She high-fives her customer and I shake my head. I thought she was the voice of reason.

Naya stops to open another pack of fake hair. "And y'all dog out men when they play those games. If you got a good man, I just think you should be straight-up."

"Good man or not," Robyn spins around in her chair, "if you dipping, you got to lie. Why ruin a good thing if he's taking care of business?"

Her eyes widen when she notices me. "Andre...Hey...What are you doing here?"

"Surprising you."

"That you did." She crosses the room and stands on her toes for a kiss. My hand lingers around her waist. I stare at her the same way I did when I first laid eyes on her in the upscale clothing store at the Lenox Mall.

Her eyes were an ember color that drew me in like the warm rays from the sun.

"Which one would you prefer?" she asked, interrupting my shortcut through the mall. She was holding up two dresses. One a navy blue, and the other a black and white dress that would hug her ample curves.

"What's the occasion?" I asked after checking to make sure she was talking to me.

"Blind date."

I put down the socks I was holding and blatantly stared. "You're kidding, right?"

Her curls bounced when she shook her head. "It's a long story. My friends think I should get back out there. So, here I am asking a strange man for fashion advice." She lowered her head and fiddled with the tags, seemingly embarrassed.

I automatically wanted to make her feel better. This woman, dressed in a designer outfit that cost a mint, was way out of my league. With a confidence I didn't know I had, I put out my hand.

"I'm Andre."

She shifted the dresses and took my hand. "Robyn."

"Now that we've met, can I ask you something?"

Her eyebrows raised. "What?"

"Could you try them on? I mean, you want a man's perspective, right?"

She smiled and winked at me over her shoulder. "Be right back."

Robyn modeled those dresses for me that day and when I met her for dinner that night, she wore the black and white dress. I was right. That dress did hug those curves. Soon after, so did I.

"Dre," Robyn snaps me back to the present. "I thought you were meeting your brother."

"No. I mean, I did. Meet Anthony," I say, ignoring the curious glances of the women around her. "I took off work for the rest of the day and wanted to see what your plans were. Maybe we can skip out together."

The women in the salon give their approval with whistles, cackles, and "Now that's nice," "Wish I had a man to 'surprise' me," and "You go, Robyn."

"Hello, ladies." I acknowledge the support.

"Now see, that's a good man, right there." Naya looks me up and down and smiles. "Some people need to recognize."

I've seen women look at men 'that way' before but it's rarely been directed at me. Robyn says that Naya has a thing for me. I think she's just being nice to the owner's man. Besides, I only have eyes for my baby.

Robyn frowns at Naya and takes my hand. "Let's talk in the back."

Robyn doesn't notice when I close and lock the door behind us. She's too busy pacing. She finally stops and crosses her arms over a pair of mouth-watering breasts. "You know I'm getting tired of Naya's mess. If she wasn't bringing in so many customers, I'd tell her to find another shop."

"Why? Because she states the obvious?" I ask, grinning. "I think it's cute."

Robyn moves in front of me. "You would. You act like you don't see her flirting with you."

I pull her close. "You jealous?"

She pushes away from me and sucks her teeth. "Ain't nobody jealous of the braid and weave queen. She needs to stop being disrespectful."

"Funny you mention respect," I say and pin a heated gaze on her. "Who sent you flowers?"

Time comes to a complete halt as Robyn turns to focus on the display of pink and red roses and rubs her neck. She bites her full lips and swallows hard.

She looks up at me and her panicked expression makes me brace for the pain of the truth. I clench my fists at the thought of another man taking Robyn from me. I don't think I can survive another heartache. I step back, afraid my hands may end up around her neck. My heart races at the thought of losing control again. I can't be responsible for what happens next.

I came to the shop seeking the truth, but standing there gazing into Robyn's eyes, I don't want to deal with reality. I need to believe that there is nobody but me and her.

My mouth feels dry and beads of sweat form on my forehead. My throat constricts and breathing becomes labored in the suffocating seconds, then minutes I'm waiting for Robyn to answer.

"Who sent them?" I manage to croak again, praying that she tells me another lie to keep my world intact.

Good man or not, you got to lie. Why ruin a good thing?

Robyn studies me and cocks her head to the side. "Those aren't mine. Ms. Maxine's husband sent them. It's their anniversary, I think."

I close my eyes, nodding. *That's a reasonable explanation.* The tension leaving my body causes me to stumble back but Robyn presses against me. She wraps her arms around me and kisses me. I savor those luscious lips, starting off gentle, but the need arises quickly, and I chase her tongue with my own.

I back her against the desk and move from her lips to the sensitive areas of her neck. I nibble on the spot where her shoulder meets, and Robyn lets out a moan.

The warmth slithering up my spine is for a different reason now. Robyn rips off my tie and removes my shirt. I pull her blouse over her head and slide the lace bra to the side exposing her breasts. I feast on the brown nipples as Robyn wraps her legs around my waist. I can feel the heat from her center and I strain against the fabric of my pants.

"You might want to lock the door," Robyn breathes into

my chest.

"Already done."

I can't believe she's letting this happen. Despite my excitement, I question the motivation for this overt display. At home, I can't borrow some nookie without giving her something in return. Now she's throwing it at me like she's trying to prove something or make up for something?

All thought goes away when Robyn loosens my belt. In one move, my slacks are around my ankles, Robyn's thong is cast aside, and I'm inside her.

In one motion, I sweep everything off the desk including those damn flowers. *Sorry, Maxine.* They crash when they hit the floor, but it doesn't stop my stroke. I lean Robyn back over the desk and pull her into me and give her all of me. All my insecurities, my desperation, and my love. I want her to feel how much I need her. I could stay here forever.

When Robyn calls out my name, I speed up the pace and take us both to heaven. The release causes my knees to buckle but I maintain my balance and stay in place until we can both catch a breath.

"Damn, baby," Robyn pants, her forehead peppered with perspiration. "Looks like we made a mess."

"We did."

Papers are strewn around the room and water drips down the desk puddling on the floor.

I help Robyn off the desk and step back to straighten my clothes. She adjusts her skirt and locates her blouse and my shirt where they were tossed in a heap.

"This was fun," she says and kisses me.

"I guess, Maxine's going to be upset."

Robyn lets out a deep sigh and smiles. "Why?"

I point to the crushed blooms. "Her flowers are ruined."

She hesitates a moment and shrugs. "No big deal. I'll replace them."

"But they were from her husband, right?" My eyes narrow on her. "Anniversary. Won't *she* think it's a big deal?"

Robyn flinches, then takes my hand. "Don't worry about that, okay? Let's talk about the way you just put it down. What came over you?"

I should confront her about what Tony saw. Make her admit that the flowers were hers. I should face reality and at least leave with my dignity intact.

But I stand there looking at this woman I've loved for the past two years. The woman I wanted to wear the ring I purchased a month ago. I was only waiting for the perfect time to ask.

Caressing her hand, I place it on my chest. "Can you feel it?" My heart beats for her. If only she can make me believe another lie.

"Stop being silly and help me clean up this mess." Robyn starts picking up flowers and I grab the trash can to help.

"This invoice is ruined," Robyn laughs and continues shifting through a stack of soggy papers.

And there it is in the trash. The one thing I can no longer pretend not to see.

I shake my head and crumble the card, releasing the dream I'd held onto far past its expiration date.

"I love you, Robyn, but I can't play this game anymore."

Panic sets in her eyes. "What do you mean? What game?"

The card reads, *Robyn, Woke up this morning with your scent on my sheets. Thanks for a wonderful evening. Looking forward to more nights to come. – William*

Robyn grips the collar of her blouse when I toss the card on the desk. "Listen, Dre. It's not what…"

"I know what you're going to say," I interrupt her and finish buttoning my shirt. She's going to tell me the flowers don't mean anything. She'll say there's no one else. All the things I desperately want to believe.

Good man or not, she told the ladies earlier. I take a deep breath and focus on being good.

"Babe," Robyn's voice is strained and causes me to pause from walking out the door. "Let me explain."

I fumble the keys in my hand but don't turn around. The dream of us can no longer support the weight of her deceptions.

"A man can only take so many lies."

.

The End

Michelle D. Rayford is a National Best-selling author whose trademark stories deal with love, marriage and the messiness that comes after saying "I Do." Her debut novel, Moment of Truth, has been applauded for its real-life characters and contemporary issues and she has short stories penned in several anthologies. Michelle lives in a Southern city with her husband and two daughters. She can be reached via her website at www.michelledrayford.com.

9

CONFESSIONS OF A DOMINATRIX

By KP Holley

"Big fella, you sure you won't be joining us? Don't let the small frame fool you. There's plenty of me to go around."

I placed my hand on my hip in full runway stance and blew a Ruby Woo'd pouty kiss at the short, balding man standing at the door. We had been playing a game of stare down that I was going to lose as this dude had barely batted an eyelid. It puzzled me that he was there in the first place. The contract didn't mention two men. As meticulous as EJ was, I knew he wouldn't mess up instructions. It wasn't uncommon for my gentlemen friends to bring an escort or guard but this dude wasn't guard material. Without my stilettos, we'd be eye-to-eye. He could be cast as Danny Devito in a movie. I stifled a laugh.

My eyes moved down the length of his round, stocky body, and landed at his crotch. "Oh, I see, you're a watcher. Miss

Cindie got your Dockers all tight." I smirked.

I won. Satisfied with seeing his fat face turn from beige to beet red, I turned my attention to the other half of the fairly odd couple who had commissioned me last minute. He was probably a foreign big wig visiting the states on business. My name and reputation were well-known internationally and in the corporate world of stocks and new technology. His booking information showed conversion from Korean currency to U.S. dollar. He wore the typical attire of a man not wanting to be recognized; long black trench coat, black hat and dark shades.

I couldn't see his face as he hurried past me into the candlelit room. He snatched the shades off and dropped them in the coat pocket and slid off his dress shoes at the door. He gave me a quick glance, but his eyes took in all of me. The corners of my mouth turned up into a wicked smile. My twenty-four-inch waist was snatched and bounded by a leather corset, which pushed my shoulders up and my 36 DDDs out. I also towered over him in height.

The sparkles in my chain-linked collar caught the light of the chandelier and illuminated my contoured cheek bones. He squinted his eyes and parted his thin lips as if to speak but instead swung around facing the man at the door. This caught me off guard. For the next few seconds my head filled with scenarios of what ifs that could send the night into a downward spiral. What if they were serial killers or traffickers? It wouldn't be the first time a sex worker was targeted. EJ kept four former linebackers turned security goons in the next room for my protection.

When the Asian man turned back around to face me, I regained control of the situation by extending my arm and pointing at a chair across the room. No words were needed. He dropped his head and scurried in that direction.

There was no hiding in the Red Room where passion was made. The crimson walls were adorned with mirrors on both sides. I watched as he removed the few articles of clothing and hung them on the coat rack next to the chair. My face lit up with anticipation once he assumed the submissive position: his back to me and his head hung low, hands on the arms of the winged chair. Whoever this guy was he knew the routine, but I would have to punish him for that stunt at the door.

Clear stilettos met hard wood when I brought my feet down with thunderous thuds. I caught a reflection of myself that made me stop mid step, almost causing me to fall. Long red tresses covered my normally pixied blue dome.

Damn it, that's what threw him off. The Asian men always requested blonde hair. Hollywood, as they called it. These guys and their fetishes.

I rolled my eyes, imagining the long drawn out talk EJ would have when he found out I grabbed "Ariel" instead of "Marilyn." He still wasn't a hundred percent on board with this lifestyle but he knew I needed this growth to be happy and whole. He understood he wasn't my pimp—no one would ever pimp me—but I loved being able to be honest with him. He assisted me investigating the guys on the dating profile who paid for my services.

* * * *

Two years ago, my life went from drab to glam when I met EJ. I was standing in front of Babe's in Downtown Arlington, Texas after having met my parents for dinner. My mom and dad flew in monthly from Oklahoma to meet as if we lived down the street, not an entire state over. Dinner with my parents had been the usual with my mom pestering me about school, men, and my career choices.

"Cynthia, you've got to do something different with your hair if you want to ever find a man," she'd said while forking fried chicken onto my plate.

I fingered my tight ringlets. She was always telling me this. Six months before, I had taken her advice and done something with my hair. That day I was wearing a long French braid. I was sweaty from the gym, but all my mom saw was wild, crazy hair. After my shower, I'd walked into the kitchen to get an apple. My mother let out the most piercing scream and dropped her tuna casserole on the marbled floor. My father came running from his recliner. They both stood in front of me with open mouths. I had taken sewing shears and my dad's razor to my signature waist-length locks, dyed my scalp black and decided it was time for me to leave the nest.

It wasn't Timbuktu, but Texas was just far enough to get a breather. I got an apartment in downtown Fort Worth, or as my mother liked to call it "The Wild Wild West." I paid a thousand dollars of my own money for a beat up car and my hair resembled something a gray cat might've coughed up. Life was good.

I shoved the plate toward her. I hadn't eaten meat in five years. She knew this. "Mom, the only hair a man is concerned about is the hair on my-"

"Okay, who wants dessert?" Dad interjected.

I looked across the table at him fiddling with the top button on his shirt and her folding and refolding her napkin. As an only child, we had this weird threesome where my mom whined and nagged, my father deflected and I ignored. I was the egg that finally took. My parents had tried for years to conceive, spending tens of thousands of dollars on IVF.

I loved them dearly and appreciated their love, attention and their money. It was their smothering me and dismissing my need to live my own life that I couldn't take.

After dinner and too tight hugs, wet kisses, and promises to call as soon as I made it home, a car service had picked them up to go to the airport. There I was standing outside, balancing the to-go box that she insisted I take and digging in my hobo for the cigarettes that I desperately needed when I was knocked on my ass by someone rushing out of the restaurant.

"Are you kidding me, dude? Damn it, I've got food everywhere." I slung a crispy, deep fried piece of bird off my jean skirt with disgust.

"My bad, love. Lemme help you with that."

My eyes followed the accented voice into the face of a dark-skinned, thick-necked, broad-chested god. When he smiled showing perfect teeth and licked his lips, I could tell he was used to women falling over him. Remembering he had just knocked me over, I jerked my arm away.

He laughed and grabbed a chicken wing out of the open box on the ground and started munching. We ended up going back into the restaurant and talking for hours over drinks. I learned he was from Louisiana, a professional football player, married and visiting Dallas for the weekend. He raised his eyebrows and asked if I needed a ride after walking me across the empty parking lot to my car. I assured him my Honda Civic was ride or die. We both laughed at the analogy. I wrote down my number on a napkin; he chuckled and pulled out his cell phone and saved it.

A month later, I got a call from an unknown number. My parents paid all my bills on time so I knew it wasn't a bill collector. The few friends I had knew to text me rather than call. I answered on the third ring. I recognized his Cajun drawl as soon as he said hello. He invited me to Atlanta for All Star Weekend. I packed everything I owned.

* * * *

A raspy cough and nasal snore snapped me out of the nostalgic moment. The Asian bastard was asleep in the chair. The smile on my face turned into a deep-set scowl.

"Dak-cho nyeon!" I yelled for him to shut up and cursed him in his native language. His head jerked upward and his eyes widened just as my open palm met the right side of his face. The violent slap sent phlegm and blood flying from his mouth.

As a dominatrix, I had experienced a level of relationships that most people wouldn't understand. I didn't get off from hurting others and it wasn't always about sex. Bondage and discipline, dominance and submission, sadism and masochism implemented power and enjoyment between all parties.

The thrash of the cymbal and run of the keys were oblivious to the two men who occupied the room with me. It provided the soundtrack to my one woman show. I swayed my hips, twirling and bouncing to the sound of my heartbeat as the adrenaline rushed to my brain. It gave me guidance in choosing the next painful pleasure I would inflict on the lucky piece of man who had deposited money into my account in exchange for me stomping on his testicles or some other ungodly act that would have him kicked out of his marital bed or church and fired from his place of employment if anyone ever found out.

Next to the window stood a double-doored eight-foot-high mahogany curio with four drawers. When I first started this dominatrix lifestyle, I bought it at a garage sale from this homely woman in Duluth. She went on and on about how her husband had handcrafted and customized it for their family and how long it had housed her grandmother's fine china. I flicked a hundred dollar bill at her and left her standing at the end of her driveway with an astonished, questionable look on her face when I told her I was single and would be using it to store my bondage toys.

The drawers with black velvet interior slid out smooth like butter. I closed my eyes and played a game of eenie meenie miney moe, choosing a silicone breathable mouth gag and jeweled flogger. Standing in front of him with my legs spread apart, I ran the back of my hand across the same cheek I had just slapped. The cool brass knuckles met warm skin. After securing the gag just tight enough, I kneaded my fingers into his shoulders, massaging the tension. The feel of his body relaxing and visibly slumping told me he was ready. I continued the massage up the back of his head and around his ears. I pretended his earlobes were udders and pulled. My pointed-shaped fingernails became tweezers pulling out strands of his thick, black hair. He stifled a moan.

I picked up the black, silk Shibari rope that lay across the back of the chair. Dropping to my knees in front of him, I used both hands to slam his parted legs together securing them at the ankles with rope.

"Nobody asked you to come out so soon." I plucked the tip of his arousal peeking out through his checkered boxer shorts. I stood back and admired my work.

I tied his hands palms up to the chair. The flaps of the jeweled flogger danced against his shins. With one swift motion, I slapped his thighs and let the flogger free like a brush to paint his chest. Tears fell from his eyes as he whimpered and moaned.

Loud voices in the hallway caused us both to leave the moment and stare toward the door. The short, fat man in the room with us jumped and took small steps away from the door right before it came crashing in. I screamed and turned to the curio to grab the hunting set I kept for knife play.

Pop pop pop!

The fat man staggered toward us. He had been shot in the back. Three masked individuals ran in waving guns and yelling for us to get on the ground. I froze. The poor Asian man looked on in horror. One of the gunmen walked toward us and stopped in front of the chair.

"What kinda freaky shit is this?" he asked, looking around at the mirrors, tools and bondage furniture. He hopped backward.

"This piece of crap pissed on me," he yelled to the other two men who replied with howling laughs.

"Well, now I have to kill him."

I screamed before I felt a hard thud in the back of my head and fell onto the bed.

When I regained consciousness, I didn't know where I was. I remembered bits and pieces of the night at the hotel. How long ago had it happened? Why hadn't EJ's security come to help? My eyes fluttered, adjusting to the brightness of the lights. I tried to open my mouth but my jaws felt like they had been stuffed with bricks. I dozed back off. I cried myself to sleep.

I dreamed of EJ and the Asian man.

"It's a sordid way to live, I'll tell you that," a female voice said.

"We're not here to judge," another voice said.

My hands were heavy. I raised them to my lips. They felt like sandpaper. I would soon find out my mouth had been duct taped. One of the voices had a face and it was staring at me. Her mouth was moving but I couldn't understand what she was saying. She explained I was in the hospital. I had been left in a warehouse for days. I couldn't recall a warehouse but I remembered being hot. I knew my name, my birth date and that Barack Obama was the president of the United States. My skin was raw in some spots. Those men had used my rope on me. I rubbed my wrists with circular motions. The other face appeared on the right side of the bed. She poked and prodded me, removing tubes and bandages.

I stuttered, "My, my phone. Can I, may I please have my phone?"

They looked at each other simultaneously.

The one on the left spoke in a soft voice. "Sweetie, you were found with no clothes on and there was no phone." She patted my hand.

"What? Naked? No one knows I'm here?" I asked, confused.

"Is there a phone I can use?" She motioned toward a phone on the bedside table.

"I can dial the number for you."

What did people do before cell phones? I only knew one number by heart, the first one I ever learned. I shook my head against the idea of calling my parents' house. I felt a warm sensation rush from my head to my toes. I closed my eyes and smiled a little.

"Let the morphine help you, sweetie," Thing One said before closing the blinds.

The next day's recuperation proved to be better. I was making strides by walking to the bathroom instead of having to use that catheter. Someone cleared their throat behind me. I grabbed the material of the flimsy hospital gown and hobbled toward the bed.

"Don't bother covering your nasty behind. I've seen it before. Hell, the whole city of Atlanta has seen it."

I spun around as best I could without falling and came face to face with a nightmare.

"Don't even think about screaming, bitch."

A nurse passed by and waved at me, stopping in the door way. "Cynthia, this is Detective Stephanie Richardson. She's been coming by to check on you. We called her when you started making improvements. We're all so glad you're up and doing better. I'll close the door so y'all can talk."

I nodded but thought Damn, this was some information she could've led with when I woke up. My face showed fear but no words came out.

We stared at each other for what seemed like hours. My eyes hurt. She didn't blink. I thought back to the short, fat man in the Red Room. I felt bile come up in my throat.

"I bet you have lots of questions. Let me help you." She threw the keypad to call the nurse's station across the room, tilted her head to the right and smiled as if she were being photographed. I had never seen her up close. She looked just like her pictures though.

"Now, you're not gonna scream or call the nurses or try any foolishness. I don't want to hurt you. Correction, I do want to hurt you but that's not what I came here for. Do you understand?" She paused.

I nodded and whispered, "Yes."

"This time you're going to listen to me." She slammed her fist on the footboard. "I asked you so many times to leave us alone. You left your nasty panties at the guard gate of my home. Did you think it was disrespectful? No, you thought it was cute, huh? Is it cute now, Cindie?" She spat my name out like it was burned food. I didn't know if she wanted me to answer. I wasn't able to form words anyway.

She rattled on, "So yeah, you're not dead. Yeah, I set you up. No, EJ doesn't know."

My face perked up at the sound of his name. She didn't notice as She continued rattling on about how an investigator had followed me for months. She couldn't believe her husband had fallen for some cheap white trash and I better hope I hadn't given him some incurable disease.

"Speak." She stepped back and crossed her arms.

I cleared my throat. I had been sleeping with this woman's husband for a year. She set me up to be assaulted and killed. It was all too much. I closed my eyes feeling a panic attack coming on. My limbs throbbed. I needed morphine. Where the hell were the nurses, Twiddle Dee and Twiddle Dum.

"EJ-."

She cut me off. "You will address him as my husband or Mr. Richardson."

I exhaled.

"Your husband is my friend. He's my confidant. He sees me as an individual in the world that wants me to be just like them. He set me free." I stopped to judge her facial expressions before continuing. "Yes, we've had sex but it's not what our relationship is based on." I hung my head in shame but continued.

"I shouldn't have violated your marriage or your home. I'm sorry. I love him but I'm not in love with him. Even if I was, EJ, uh, your husband would never accept me as his woman. My lifestyle is not one that has limits or boundaries. I give him freedom, too."

"By doing all that freaky shit, you feel like you're freeing him?"

For the first time in days, I laughed.

"He doesn't let me do any of those things to him. He's not into BDSM. He protects me." I began to cry. I looked down at the bruises on my arms. He hadn't protected me though.

As if reading my mind, she answered my unasked question,

"I made sure to give the security detail the night off. I can't believe he was using our money to fund this bull."

"You wanted those men to kill me and what about the guys?

What happened to them?"

"Mr. Nagoya and his mute friend were caught up, unfortunately." She waved her hand dismissing the thought. "It was a business decision. However, if I wanted you dead, you'd be dead. I already sent Mr. Richardson a message from you saying you're moving on to some other sucker that will support your sick, twisted lifestyle. Listen to me. If you care about EJ at all, don't ever contact him again."

She dug inside her designer bag and pulled out my cell.

"Oh, and your mom has left you tons of voicemails. She

wants you to eat and use a keratin shampoo for your hair." She laughed at her joke and walked out of the door leaving it open.

A year later
Cozumel, Mexico

I wrapped one bronzed leg around my bed guest and allowed the other to caress the hair at the nape of my neck. The sun shined through the open bay window of the bungalow. The best part of waking up in a tropical paradise was having someone next to you to share it with. Well, in my case two someones. I had spent the last week being the Oreo cream to an adventurous, French husband and wife duo.

"Ahhh, Marcella we hate to see you go. Stay and travel with us. Be our unicorn," said Bryce in a thick, French accent while licking behind my knee caps.

"You plead a good case, sir, but I'm an eagle not a canary." Renee, his wife, nuzzled her face into my breasts. We shared a smile before I untangled myself from the intimate body pretzel and got up to shower.

"Marcella, the Americans are such brutes. Every time the news airs there is crime on the television," Bryce said while reaching for the remote to change the station.

"Oh my, Gosh, turn that up!"

The reporter was speaking in Spanish. The words scrolling across the screen read, "Falcons QB, EJ Richardson Murdered in his Home, Christmas Day."

The news cut to a clip of his wife, Stephanie, being led out of their home in handcuffs. I guess I had been lucky she let me live, which was more than I could say for EJ.

"Maybe I'll take you up on that offer after all," I said to

Bryce and Renee who just replied with broad smiles and lustful eyes.

The End

KP Holley *is a native of New Orleans and lives in the Dallas-Fort Worth area with her husband and three daughters. She earned a Bachelor's of Science degree in mass communications from Jackson State University in Jackson, Mississippi. Confessions of a Dominatrix is a prologue to My Heart's First Wish from the Brown Girls Anthology, All I Want For Christmas.*

10

SOMEONE I USED TO KNOW

By Tracie Momie

The sound of her laughter made me smile. She was excited about tonight and for the first time in almost a year, she seemed to be back to her old self.

I watched as she laughed and danced around the kitchen while Alexa played 90s R&B music. This was the woman I fell in love with seven years ago.

I'd only caught glimpses of her in the past year. The happy, bubbly and affectionate woman I married, had been replaced with someone moody, melancholy, and in a constant state of grief. Nothing I did or said improved her mood. But when I'd told her about my promotion and hinted that we would have to move to Houston, she was all for it. She wanted to get away from Atlanta. Get away from her family and friends. Away from their sympathetic remarks and piteous glances. She wanted to start over where nobody knew she was broken. These were *her* words, not mine.

I never considered her broken. We'd talked about having children one day but it wasn't a deal breaker for me. I just wanted her. I tried to reassure her of this every time she got pregnant only to lose the baby in the first trimester. It happened a total of six times before the doctor told her she wouldn't be able to conceive a baby on her own. He'd suggested surrogacy and even adoption, but my wife refused to consider those options. Instead, she retreated within herself and away from me.

After we moved to Houston, she kept busy by decorating and organizing the new house. She'd even found a part-time job at a law firm downtown. I could see an awakening happening, but it wasn't until she joined a book club with some ladies from work that she really started to come back to life. She'd always enjoyed reading but now she had a group of girlfriends to discuss the books with; although I got the feeling they did more laughing and drinking than actually discussing the books.

But I was happy that she was happy. Because that happiness was seeping back into our marriage.

It was her turn to host the book club meeting. I helped her set up but was told I had to disappear for a few hours. Apparently, there was a hard and fast rule about 'no men' at their meetings. I knew it was probably due to the fact that they talked about men and didn't want us to know.

I'd moved the sofa, loveseat, and recliner closer together so that the furniture formed a circle. This would create a more intimate setting for their book discussion *and* gossip.

"Is there anything else I can do before you kick me out?" I teased.

She laughed. "Babe, I'm not kicking you out. You just can't be here during my meeting," she batted her eyelashes at me.

"I'm pretty sure that's the same thing." I laughed.

She pretended to think about it for a second. "No, I'm pretty sure that's two different things."

I grabbed her around the waist and pulled her to me.

"What time should I come back for my private book discussion?" I waggled my eyebrows.

"Sean, stop! People will be arriving soon." She giggled and tried half-heartedly to free herself from my grip.

"But *Kayla*, I want to kiss you!" I whined.

She bit her lip and looked up at me before locking her arms around my neck. "One kiss," she said slowly.

I leaned in closer and just as my lips touched hers, we were interrupted by the sound of the doorbell.

"No!" I groaned.

"Hush." She laughed as she pulled away from me. "Come back at 9:30 and we'll pick up where we left off," she promised as she left the kitchen to answer the front door.

A moment later, I heard Kayla and another voice echoing in the foyer.

"Hey, girl! Come on in. Did you have a hard time finding it?" Kayla asked.

"No, not at all. The directions were perfect. Am I the first one here?" the woman asked.

"Yes, but that's fine, everybody will start showing up soon," Kayla assured her.

"Your home is beautiful," the woman complimented.

"Thank you. Let me say goodbye to my husband and I'll give you a tour. You can bring the wine to the kitchen," Kayla instructed as her voice got closer.

I reached over and grabbed my car keys from the hook near the refrigerator, and when I turned around Kayla entered the kitchen with a woman following closely behind.

"Babe, I want you to meet someone." She smiled at me.

When the woman looked up and our eyes locked, everything started to move in slow motion. Her eyes widened, probably mirroring my own. And the bottle she held slipped through her fingers and crashed to the floor.

The sound snapped me out of my catatonic state and I immediately reached for Kayla. I looked down at the shards of glass and the liquid that was spreading across the kitchen floor.

"Oh my, God, Kayla I'm so sorry!" the woman shrieked as she covered her mouth.

"Girl, it's okay, be careful. Let me get something to wipe that up." Kayla hurried from the kitchen.

I opened the pantry door and pulled out a broom to sweep up the glass. When Kayla returned with a towel, the woman insisted on cleaning up the wine herself as she squatted.

"You okay?" I asked Kayla. She nodded and shrugged as she glanced in the woman's direction.

"That should be fine. I'll sweep up the rest of the glass," I offered.

Kayla took the towel to the laundry room, and I made sure the floor was glass free. I avoided making further eye contact with the woman.

"Okay, so, babe this is Kim. She's an attorney at the firm. Kim this is my husband, Sean, and he's on his way out." Kayla winked at me.

"Nice to meet you, Kim," I said formally. "I guess I should go, I don't want to get in trouble." I smiled and kissed Kayla's cheek before I headed out of the kitchen.

"Nice to meet you," I heard Kim's voice when I was halfway out the door.

I sat in my car, raised my shaking hands and put the keys in the ignition. I pulled out of the driveway and headed to the sports bar right outside our neighborhood. I was meeting one of my neighbors from the Homeowners Association Board for a drink. Keith was a cool guy. We'd hit it off immediately and were on the way to becoming good friends.

"Hey man, how's it going?" Keith greeted me when I approached him at the bar. "Whoa, you look like you could use a drink." He raised an eyebrow.

Was it that obvious? I hoped Kayla hadn't noticed.

"Yes, a drink is exactly what I need," I agreed.

I ordered a Jameson on the rocks.

"Okay, what happened?" Keith asked, not wasting any time.

We hadn't known each other long, but I felt like I could trust him. And even if I couldn't, I needed to talk to someone and he was there. After the bartender poured my drink, I took a sip and winced as the liquor burned the back of my throat. I looked over at Keith before I spoke.

"There are over seven billion people in the world, seven continents and countless countries, right?" I asked.

It was a rhetorical question but Keith answered anyway. "That sounds about right."

"Can you explain how - with those kind of odds - how is it possible that my ex-girlfriend showed up in my kitchen tonight?"

Keith's eyes widened. "What? How did she. . . oh, tonight is your wife's book club thing, right? She's in your wife's book club?" He came to the conclusion rather quickly.

I just nodded and took another sip of my drink.

"You didn't know she was in the book club?" he asked.

"Hell no!"

"Hold up, I'm still not following. How long ago was she your girlfriend? Why does this matter?" Keith asked genuinely confused.

I sighed and recalled the story from my past.

"Kim and I started dating in our senior year of high school. We lost our virginity to each other on the night of our senior prom. We moved to Atlanta together and attended Georgia State. We'd mapped out our entire future. We were going to get our degrees, get our dream jobs, get married, travel the world and then have kids. *In that order*. She was my best friend and the love of my life, and I couldn't imagine a future without her." I took another sip of my drink.

"She got pregnant in our junior year of college," I continued. "We were almost done with the first big thing on our list. Having a baby wasn't next on the list. Having a baby was *way* down on the list, and would ruin everything. We were too young. And I told her so. She'd wanted to keep the baby. But I pressured her into getting an abortion. No one else knew. Not even our parents or close friends. Things were never the same after that. She resented me. She resented herself for giving into my demand. When we graduated, she stayed in Georgia to start law school and I returned to Chicago to get my MBA. Tonight, was the first time I'd seen her in over ten years."

"Damn," Keith replied after I finished my story.

"Damn is right. I never told Kayla about her. Or the abortion. Especially since…" I almost told him about our struggle to get pregnant but decided I'd shared enough.

Keith didn't push me to finish. "Are you going to tell Kayla?" he asked.

I shrugged. "I don't know. For all I know, Kim is at my house telling her right now."

"That would be bad. Very bad," Keith decided.

"No shit," I agreed.

"So, how was it seeing her after all this time? Do you think you still have feelings for her?" Keith asked.

I wanted to say no. I wanted to say it with conviction and confidence. After all, I was a married man; a married man in love with his wife. But I'd be lying if I said seeing her didn't have an effect on me. A flood of memories came back to me the moment I looked in her eyes. I'd always felt my time with Kim had ended too soon because of my stupidity. After our break-up, I'd regretted the abortion. Regretted how stubborn and callous I had been. Over the years, I'd thought about Kim and wondered how my life would have been different if I'd married her. I'd probably be a father by now. But I wouldn't change my life with Kayla for anything.

"I think I was just shocked, you know? I never expected to see her again. Especially here of all places," I admitted.

"Did she say anything or remember who you were?"

I chuckled. "She dropped the bottle of wine she was holding and it shattered on the kitchen floor."

"Are you serious? But she didn't say anything out of line, did she?" Keith questioned.

"Nah, we both pretended like it was our first-time meeting," I said sadly. I hated that I'd done that. It felt like a betrayal to Kayla.

Keith groaned. "That might come back to bite you in the ass."

"I know. I know. I was just so shocked and it wasn't the right time to open up that whole can of worms."

I also didn't want to disturb Kayla's peace or destroy the friendships she was building. Her book club was saving her life and by default, our marriage.

"You've got to come clean," Keith advised. "Trust me, I know how secrets, even unintentional ones can eat away at you and eventually destroy your relationships,"

I glanced at him as he launched into a story about how he'd cheated on his ex-wife with her sister before they were married. They'd agreed it was a mistake and made a promise to never tell his wife about it. But it came out after an ugly fight between the two sisters. His wife had left him and had taken their nine-month-old son with her. He'd remarried and had another child but his relationship with his son from his first marriage was strained because of the ex.

"Sorry to hear that, man," I remarked.

"Ah...it's my own damn fault." He shrugged. "I just think you should tell your wife. I mean at least in your case, it was over before you ever met her."

For some reason, I didn't think it would matter. Once I told her *why* we broke up, I knew Kayla would find it hard to forget that I'd convinced a woman to get an abortion.

Keith and I ordered another round of drinks and talked for a little while longer before I decided to head home. When I got home, the kitchen was spotless and Kayla was in our bedroom.

"Honey, I'm home!" I called out.

"Hey. I was just about to text you." She smiled. I considered that a good sign.

"Well, I'm here now." I winked at her. "How did the book club meeting go?" I asked not sure I wanted to know.

"It went really well, everybody actually read the book this time." She laughed. "You know after you left, Kim said she remembered you from high school but that you probably didn't remember her."

My heart thundered in my chest. Now was the time to come clean. "I don't-" I started to speak but Kayla kept talking.

"She's actually transferring to the New York office. Her husband got a job there, so they leave in a few weeks. Did I tell you they have a son named, Sean?"

I lost my balance and fell to the edge of the bed.

"Are you okay? How much did you have to drink?" Kayla asked as her eyebrows raised slightly.

"I only had two. I tripped over my shoelace," I lied and prayed she didn't hear the way my voice shook. "How old is Kim's son?" I asked nonchalantly. I was being a masochist. I knew for a fact she'd had an abortion but *what if* - what if she'd gotten pregnant afterward, before we broke up and didn't tell me?

"Huh? Oh, I think he's like two or three. Man, I'm going to miss her," Kayla said and I let go of the breath I'd been holding.

"I was about to get in the shower and was thinking maybe we could finish what you started in the kitchen earlier." She winked.

"Would you like some company in the shower?" I walked over and pulled her into my arms.

"I guess it would be the responsible thing to do, water

conservation is important." She laughed.

We took turns washing each other in the shower, *thoroughly*, and after some extensive foreplay, I made love to my wife late into the night.

As Kayla lay asleep next to me, I looked down at her face and made a decision. Now that Kim would no longer be a part of my wife's life, there was no need to bring up unnecessary drama. While it might ease *my* conscience for Kayla to know my secret, it would no doubt hurt her. I shared a history with Kim but Kayla was my future and some things were better left in the past.

The End

Tracie Momie is an author and freelance graphic designer. She is the author of five novels, including her latest release Love or Something Like That. She currently resides in Houston with her husband and two kids. Visit her at www.traciemomie.com

11

BETRAYED

By Yolonda Attaglo

Louise

I set William's plate on the dining room table. He sits in the same seat all the time. It never changes. Never varies. His plate must sit directly in the center of the placemat. His glass always has to be on the right – atop a coaster. Fork on the right. Knife on the left.

I study my set-up, make sure it's perfect, then glance toward the clock on my dining room wall. I swear my husband is slower than molasses. Running behind a grown man is not my idea of a good time.

Even still, I walk toward the stairs, ready to call out to tell him his breakfast is going to get cold. As I move closer to the staircase, I hear a faint ringing sound that makes me stop in my tracks and scan the room trying to locate the source.

I follow the ringing into William's office and open the top drawer of his desk. Under some papers, I see a cell phone that I'd never seen before.

I stand in between confusion and perplexity, staring at it ring. No name or number appears on the caller ID. In the midst of debating whether to answer it, the ringing stops. I place the cell phone back in the drawer, under the papers, as if it were never touched, close the drawer and head out of the office.

But I barely make it to the stairs before it rings again.

Curiosity takes over me. I hurry back, fling open the drawer, snatch up the phone and answer.

"Hello."

I'm greeted by silence. Then, a click.

Now, not only do I have questions, I am pissed. I ascend the stairs faster than I thought possible. I move with fire in my steps. My emotion is on ten. A thin mist covers my forehead and distress and agitation brew in the depths of my stomach. I reach my destination and stand outside the door. Thinking. Contemplating. Reflecting. Planning the exact words I want to spew when I see his face.

"I am looking forward to it, too."

The enthusiasm and strength in William's voice snaps me back to now and stops me from turning the knob. I wonder who he's talking to and what the hell he's looking forward to. I haven't heard him sound so eager and interested in so long, I almost forgot what it sounds like. Whoever he's talking to definitely has his undivided attention – something I haven't had in months. I can't help but feel a little jealous.

"Okay, I'll see you tomorrow morning."

I stand outside the door – waiting. Listening. Waiting. Waiting for what? I don't know. Maybe I'm hoping to hear something else – something that will prove that I'm just acting crazy and that William loves me with everything in his soul. I yearn to hear something to prove that I am his one and only.

I shake away those feelings and open the door, ready to curse him out. When I see him, I say, "Hey, are you coming down for breakfast?"

I don't know why I lost my nerve. Maybe because William was always so agitated lately and I wasn't in the mood for a fight.

He shakes his head without looking my way. "No. I'll get something at the office."

It takes a whole lot for me to maintain my composure. "Who were you talking to on the phone?"

"No one," he replies.

I ball up my fist and envision myself punching him in his lying eye. "I heard you say you would see someone tomorrow morning."

He dismisses me nonchalantly while he continues to tie his tie. He is wearing the navy blue and black silk one with the paisley print. It's his favorite. I bought it for him for his birthday last year. I suddenly have the urge to choke him with it.

"That? Oh…that…that was just a client. I'm sorry this is such short notice, but I have to leave first thing tomorrow morning. This just came up. The boss wants me to meet with a big client and wine and dine him."

William must be crazy. I am this close to kicking him in his bad kneecap. I'm the same woman whose food he eats. I think he forgot. He just doesn't know who he's playing with.

"Don't they give you some kinda advance notice before they send you on outta town business trips?" I ask, preparing for the lie that I know is about to come out of his mouth.

"Listen, when the boss tells me to go, I have to go. I'm not going to say no and do anything to jeopardize my job. You want to keep living in this big house and in this fancy neighborhood, don't you? You have a lot of nerve to question me."

William grabs his suit jacket and brushes past me. I should stick my foot out and trip him. I'm surprised that he doesn't break something as hard as he slams the door.

I stand in the middle of our bedroom, dumbfounded, my heart draped in doubt and my mind clothed in suspicion.

Before I discovered the secret phone and long before I was hung up on, I noticed William changing. His body language. His actions. His conversation. He has become more distant. We have become more disconnected. And I have become more detached.

William used to be so kind. Loving. Caring. Nothing like who he is today.

I remember when I first saw William in the café. His hair was precisely cut and edged up just right. His thin mustache was skillfully trimmed. I thought he was extremely handsome. I almost fell over when he approached me. I had stopped in to pick up my usual morning latte and he was at the counter looking good and smelling fine. His extremely fit physique and milk chocolate complexion made my toes curl. When he turned to me and asked the time, my stomach started flipping and flopping. He had the whitest set of teeth I'd ever seen. I spoke slowly, making sure I didn't stutter, mispronounce any words or say out loud how fine I thought he truly was.

That was seven years ago. A lot has happened since then. We got married. I gave him a son, Emmanuel. We purchased a home and seven months ago, my marriage started falling apart.

These days, William is away on business more often and for longer periods of time. He doesn't communicate with me at all when he's gone – not a phone call, not a text message, not a postcard, not a letter-in-a-bottle or a message by carrier pigeon. Nothing. He doesn't even call to check on Manuel. I used to call him often when he was away, but he was always abrupt and evasive during our conversations. There was one too many of those 'let me call you backs'. I felt like I shouldn't even bother. I stopped calling and he never started, and so here we are. Separated and Removed. Isolated and at a crossroads. I try to bond and connect with him, but he is always too busy or too preoccupied or gone.

I have planned date nights, picnics and movie nights, but he was always working and/or just not home. The frequent business trips, the distance and aloofness all made me consider hiring a private investigator, but I am even unsure about that. Half of me feels like if I have to hire somebody to spy on him, then I don't need to be with him. But the other half wants to confirm what I feel I already know. The writing is on the wall. Anyone can look in and clearly see what is going on. William is seeing someone else and I am not sure what I want to do about it.

There's a part of me that is hoping we're just hitting our seven year hurdle and that he's still faithful and until I see concrete proof, I'm still holding on to hope. I think that's why I haven't broken completely down yet.

I keep seeing the same movie replaying in my head. We used to be so easy and uncomplicated, now, even a five minute conversation is a struggle. William has become difficult to love and even harder to live with. I wonder why I'm here, and why am I choosing to stay.

****

Four days. That's how long it's been since I talked to my husband. He has not bothered to call at all since he left for his trip.

I was lucky enough to secure a babysitter for a few hours today and made a decision to be selfish and engage in some much needed retail therapy. I am hoping it will provide me with a momentary distraction. I need to think about something other than William and our crumbling marriage for just for a brief moment.

I was walking through the men's section, on my way to jewelry when a voice stops me.

"Hello, excuse me."

I turn and look over my shoulder. "Yes?"

"I was wondering if you can help me," he says, smiling.

"Oh, I am sorry. I don't work here," I say, as I start to walk away.

Following me, he says, "I didn't think you did." He flashes a grin. "I like your sense of style."

I don't know why I suddenly feel flattered. Probably because it has been months since William paid me a compliment. "Thank you. What did you need help with?"

"I need to pick out a dress shirt, slacks and tie and I don't know where to start."

"Okay, come on. Let's get you looking good," I say, smiling. It feels pretty good to know my opinion and ideas matter to someone.

I take some pants and button down shirts off the rack and pair them together. He likes some of my suggestions and others he isn't that enthused with. I don't approve of anything he tries to put together. I don't know where he got his sense of fashion, but he needs to give it back – quickly.

"What about this?" I say, holding up a pair of dark gray dress slacks, a lighter-colored purple shirt and a purple, gray and black tie.

He nods his approval. "Yeah, I like it."

"Great," I say, feeling really good about my accomplishment.

"Thank you for your help." He takes the outfit.

"You're welcome."

As we prepare to depart, I wonder if he will wait a few seconds to watch me as I walk away. A small part of me is hoping he will. It will feel good to know I'm the focus of someone's interest, even if it is only temporary.

I thought about how that shade of purple will complement his caramel complexion. I wanted to ask him what event he purchased the outfit for. I wonder if it is for a wedding or graduation. I wonder who his date will be and what she'll be wearing. I wonder if he'll glide her across the dance floor and if she'll be so smitten with his movement and his words that she'll give herself to him. I wonder if he is a counterfeit. An illusion. The morning after she surrenders to him, will she find anything in him that she recognizes?

"Excuse me," he says just as I was leaving.

I turn to face him. There is an awkward moment of silence between us.

"Can I take you to lunch? Just a friendly lunch to repay you for all your help."

I pause. My mind screams 'yes', but my heart screams 'hell no'. After a long pause, I reply, "I don't think that would be a good idea, but thanks for the invitation."

"Okay. I understand."

As he turns to walk away, I start to consider his proposition. I gently grab his arm. "I don't even know your name."

"Myles."

In that instant, with my hand on his arm, I want desperately to take him up on his offer. Really, what harm could it do? It's only lunch.

"Myles, on second thought, I will join you for lunch."

****

Lunch turned into dinner and dinner turned into everything else. Everything that I wanted from my husband, but couldn't get, Myles gives to me.

With Myles, I feel alive again. Almost five months have passed since Myles and I met and as I lay resting in his arms, my hair still damp and my pillow smelling of sweat and passion, I can't help but wonder how this story will end. I stare into the blackness, exhausted from carrying the weight of ecstasy, shame, euphoria and guilt on my shoulders. I want to tell Myles to let me go, but instead, hear "Hold me tighter," spill from my lips. It is my own desire for pleasure that consumes me.

I need Myles. I need him to explore my body. I need his hands, his mouth. I need his skin to touch mine. I need to feel his breath on my neck. I need Myles and I need Myles to need me. My soul feels bad. My body feels good. It is finally getting the attention it craved.

I give so much of myself away to Myles, more than I even

realize. When he speaks, I hang on his every word. His greatest gift is making me feel special. Loved. Even if it is a lie.

Loving him was not part of the plan. I *think* I love him. Maybe. When we began, I pleaded for him to tell me the truth, now I beg him to tell me the lies that men tell women – "You're the only one," "We will be together forever," and the big one, "I love you." Now, I prefer the lies. I don't want to know if I am sharing him with someone else. I don't want to know the truth anymore. It is easier to live with the lies. Maybe I really *don't* love him. Maybe that's why it's easier.

I am a woman who is a wife and a mother, who has a family. When I look in the mirror, there is nothing I see that I recognize. Betrayal, lies, emptiness, deceit – that's what I've become.

It becomes easier every day to close my eyes and wrap myself in Myles. In his affection, his laughter, his strength, his excitement, his enthusiasm for me. The life that I share with Myles distracts me from my own reality. When we are together time is still. All time is this time. This moment. Now is the only moment that matters.

****

I stare at the little white stick. And the plus sign.

I thought we were being careful. We used condoms every time. There's no way I can even explain my way out of this or hide it. As much as I lust for Myles, the thought of losing my family horrifies me.

This is unequivocally, the end of my marriage and my family. In my heart, I know it's too late. Too much has happened. William and I have only had sex a few times in the last couple months so I am sure Myles is the father.

Sitting on the edge of the bathtub, staring at the little white stick makes my stomach churn. Holding this little stick and all the power it possesses suffocates me. This little white stick holds my future in its hands.

I call Myles, anxious and nervous, "Myles, we need to talk."

"Okay. You sound upset. What's going on?"

I blurt out the words haphazardly. "Myles….Myles, I'm pregnant."

I wait for a reaction. I want to hear Myles reassure me. I need him to tell me that everything will be okay. I want him to be excited at the prospect of me delivering a baby born out of our desire and thirst for each other, even though I'm not sure if me keeping this baby is even an option.

"Pregnant. Aww man. That wasn't part of the plan."

Confused and disturbed, I say, "Plan? What plan?"

"I saw you at the store and you looked sad. I saw your wedding ring and hoped your husband was the reason why. You were dressed nice so I knew you had a couple dollars and I needed things here and there…"

Suddenly feeling regretful, I say, "I only gave you money because I cared about you and wanted to help you."

Trying not to let him hear the hurt and disappointment in my voice, I whisper, "Wh-what are you saying? This whole thing between us was about you getting money from me?"

"Yeah. When you offer it I take. I mean I think you're a nice person, but I need money to live," he said casually.

My mind is in shambles. "I don't even understand how this could have happened. We used condoms every time." I think I went there because I was too hurt to address the fact that I'd been straight conned.

"There were a few times when the condom slipped off," Myles confesses. The words fall from his mouth so easily.

"What?"

"I don't like using condoms."

What the hell? My stomach is hurting even more now.

I yell, "What! And why are you just telling me this now?"

I don't know how to process this whole thing. I think I'm in shock. He doesn't care that he set out to purposely destroy my marriage. My family. His attitude and disposition is so cavalier. Nonchalant. Insensitive. He sickens me.

This is the biggest lie I've ever allowed myself to be told and believe. The most damaging lie. The most life-shattering lie. I don't know what to say, so I stay silent.

"You don't seem like the abortion type and I'm not taking care of a baby. You can tell your husband it's his. I don't care, but if you don't want your husband to see the video, then it would be a good idea for you to give me $10,000 by Friday. Today is Tuesday so you have three days. That's enough time for you to get the money."

Moving from devastation to sorrow to fury, I yell, "What video and how the hell do you think I'm supposed to give you $10,000 in three days? And why is there a video?"

"I told you I needed things so why wouldn't there be a video? And I don't care how you get it. That's not my problem."

I prepare to enter into a state of rage, but the dial tone stops me before I can get the first curse word out.

I slide to the floor in tears.

William

Meeting Louise was the happiest day of my life. I can still remember what she was wearing in the café on that Monday morning six years ago. She had on a knee length, form fitting black dress, navy blue high heels and she was carrying a navy blue handbag. Her perfume was subtle. Her makeup applied just right. Her hair was flawless. She was beautiful. The most beautiful woman I'd ever seen.

I was apprehensive, but I approached her anyway. I was hoping she'd agree to a dinner date and I was ecstatic when she did. Eight months later, I asked Louise to marry me. I took my position as provider seriously. I have done everything I could possibly do to make ends meet and provide for my family.

I'm not sure how much longer this whole thing is going to last. I want to be honest with Louise, come clean and tell her the truth, but I can't. Not yet. I just need a little more time.

The loud ring interrupts my thoughts and jolts me back into realty.

Reaching for the phone, I say, "Hello."

"Hi. I was just checking to make sure you were all packed for the trip."

"Yes, I'm packed."

"The plane leaves tomorrow morning at 6 a.m. I will meet you at the airport at four. Is Louise taking you to the airport?"

"No. I'm taking a taxi."

"Does Louise still think all these trips we're taking are business trips?"

Filled with misery and discontent, I reply, "She doesn't know that you are traveling with me. She thinks I'm alone."

"Oh, I see. When are you gonna tell her?"

Feeling pressured, I snap, "I don't know. Soon though."

"You said that last month. Soon! I'm not going to wait around forever!"

I sigh. "I know. Just give me a little more time."

"If you don't want to tell your wife, maybe I should."

Trying to reassure her, I say, "No. I'll tell her. When we get back from this trip. I promise. I'll tell her."

All I heard was, "You better," before she slammed the phone down. All these months of traveling back and forth with Erica, hiding this secret from my wife, has torn me apart. I should have told Louise, but I didn't want her to see me like this. Vulnerable. Helpless. I have always been the one taking care of everything and now to be the one who needs help... I feel inadequate. I feel like she will think I'm not enough for her.

I should have told Louise long ago that I was sick. Traveling back and forth for medical treatment all these months, with my assistant, has ruined my marriage. I know Louise feels neglected and abandoned. I should have given my wife the opportunity to be there for me, but I didn't. I chose to let Erica comfort me. Encourage me. Uplift me. Play the role in my life that Louise should have been playing. It's my fault. I let Erica believe things I should not have because I was caught up in the moment. I love my wife and want to keep my family together, but in my heart, I know it's too late. Too much has happened.

I should have been more careful. There's no way I can even explain my way out of this or continue to hide it. Erica won't let me. This is unequivocally, the end of my marriage and my family. I can't hide my affair with Erica or her pregnancy much longer. I am the father of her baby.

A tear trickles down my cheek as I know I have to come clean tonight.

****

Louise

I open the front door and see William sitting at the dining room table looking disheveled and dismal. I am more nervous than I've ever been in my life. How can I face my husband, the man I've shared my hopes and dreams with, and tell him that I am pregnant with another man's baby? I don't even know where to find the words.

William looks up at me. His eyes are blood shot red and puffy. Why is he crying? I don't ever think I've seen him cry before. This is definitely going to be a difficult conversation.

"Hi," I say, turning quickly so I don't have to look into his eyes.

"Hi," he replies, his voice cracking.

"How was your trip?" I ask, attempting to make small talk.

He replies, "Listen Louise, sit down. I have something to say."

My heart immediately starts racing. Did Myles tell him? Today is only Thursday. Did Myles get antsy and decide to tell him early? Pulling the chair out slowly, I sit down, not really sure what to expect. William stares at me with tears in his eyes.

"Louise, I love you. I love you and Manuel more than anything in this world."

I gaze at him intensely, anxiously awaiting his next few words.

"Louise, all of these business trips I've been taking are not really business trips. I've been traveling to see a doctor in Ohio.

147

He specializes in my condition."

Puzzled, I sit still and quiet, trying to understand what he's saying to me.

"What condition?" I ask, frowning and bewildered.

With tears welling up in his eyes, he says, "I have an Anaplastic Astrocytoma. It's a cancerous brain tumor. Dr. Harrison is the best. I have been going to him for treatments. He has been using radiation to try to shrink it. Louise, there's no cure for it."

As he continues to explain, he mentions the secret cell phone. I didn't tell him I knew anything about it. He said it was a cell phone he purchased so the doctor's office could contact him. He instructed them to only to speak to him and not to leave messages.

Oh my, God. I can't believe this. I don't know what to say. My husband is sick and may be dying and I'm carrying another man's baby. I want to throw up. How can I tell William what I've done? I am a horrible human being. I am devastated. I put my face in my hands and cry the hardest cry I've ever cried.

William pulls me to him and holds me close. He rubs my back and whispers in my ear, "Everything will be okay."

After calming me down, he gently lifts my face. "Louise, I have something else to tell you."

My God, there's more. Tears streaming down my face, I ask, "What else could there be?"

Holding my hands in his, he says, "I wasn't going to my treatment appointments alone. My assistant went with me."

"Erica?" I reply, sobbing.

"Yes."

"Why? Why didn't you tell me?

"I was hoping it wasn't really serious and when I found out

it was, I didn't want you to think I was weak or inadequate."

"What?" I say feeling even worse.

"I felt like I couldn't take care of you the way I should."

Grabbing his face, I pull him toward me. "You have always taken care of us and I love you for it."

William takes a deep breath and puts his head down. After a few seconds, he looks me in my eyes.

"Erica and I have been having an affair. She's pregnant."

My heart drops into my stomach. I glare at him, disgusted. Shocked. Appalled. I can't bring myself to say anything more in this moment. I wonder what he will say when I tell him I'm carrying another man's baby.

"Louise, I'm so sorry. I didn't mean for this to happen. I love you. I want to make our marriage work. Please don't leave me."

He grabs me, hugs me and sobs on my shoulder. He holds me tight. Close. He doesn't know he's not the only one carrying the weight of secrets, lies and betrayal.

Rubbing his back, I decide, since we're confessing, it's my turn. "William. William look at me."

He lifts his head slowly. His eyes puffy and swollen. His cheeks, hot and wet. He looks at me.

"I have something I have to tell you, too."

His eyes fill with worry. "What is it?"

"I've been having an affair, too…and I'm pregnant."

The color drains from William's face. I see the hurt and disappointment in his soul. He doesn't say a word. He stands up from the table and slowly walks away. I jump up and follow him down the hall. He stops abruptly and starts yelling and screaming and calling me a whore and a slut.

"Are you kidding me?" I say. He has the nerve to call me

names when he's done the exact same thing.

The night was explosive. William and I had a knockdown, drag out. Shouting. Weeping. Wrath. Calm conversation. Honesty. Hope. And finally, reconciliation.

That was several months ago. Counseling has helped William and me move forward together. Our marriage is stronger than ever.

Myles disappeared not long after I told him I was pregnant. Once I informed him that my husband knew all about us, there was no reason for him to hang around. No prospect of a dollar.

William stood by me during my entire pregnancy and was in the delivery room. I was ecstatic when baby Lyric's DNA test proved that William was her biological father. Lyric is a beautiful, happy baby.

Erica gave birth to a baby boy she named Westley. To keep the peace in my marriage, I learned to coexist with her. She wanted William and made that known, but William made it known that his focus was on me, our family and rebuilding our marriage. When William called Erica about Westley, she always took the opportunity to try to rekindle what they had, after he told her in my presence, on more than one occasion, that their affair was over.

Finally, on one of her whiny calls, I decide that I have had enough.

Snatching the telephone from William, I snap, "Listen Erica, William is only dealing with you because of Westley. We are together and we are staying together. He doesn't want you."

"I love him and I'm not gonna stop. He's the father of my baby." Her voice reeks of desperation.

"And he's MY husband," I shout back. "He has made it perfectly clear whatever nonsense y'all had going on is over."

"No, it's not over," she replies.

"Oh yes it is. Let me tell you something, you better be careful playing with me. You don't know who you're dealing with. Consider yourself warned," I say, slamming the phone down.

William is still being treated for the brain tumor. It seems as if the treatments are working. The tumor is shrinking. He still travels out of state, but not as often. I am the one accompanying him on the trips now.

Not long after Westley was born, Erica became very depressed. I'm not sure if postpartum depression set in or if she was depressed because William did not leave me for her. She refused to do much of anything for herself, including cook, so when I cooked dinner, I would send food over to her. I told William I felt sorry for her. William thought it was a kind gesture. Eventually, the two of us agreed to care for Westley full time because Erica was an emotional wreck and kept spiraling downward.

After some time, Erica fell ill and died. It was quite unexpected. Her family chalked it up to natural causes. They never conclusively found out her cause of death. Perhaps it had something to do with those homemade meals I sent over for all those months, but to be honest, we'll truly never know.

After her death, her body was cremated. And my husband and I finally lived happily ever after.

The End

Yolonda Attaglo *has a passion for books, writing and travel. Check out her debut, self-published work,* her darkest hour, *penned under the name Yolonda Terrell-McMillon. Available at Amazon and online at Barnes and Nobel.*

12

SPOIL ME DADDY

By T.L. Jackson

I've always loved the finer things like Burberry and Gucci. I may be only 18 years old, but my taste is refined. No 'Forever 21' labels for me. No thank you, that's basic bitch shit. I pride myself in staying draped in nothing less than Supreme.

I can't help it that I like the flashy looks and the chill styles. Can't a girl have it all? Well, she should. I should, so I do.

I looked over to my therapist as she waited for me to continue my thoughts out loud instead of in my head. Her pen was in her right hand ready to write. Guess I got caught up justifying myself within my mind.

"Michelle, we only have five minutes left," she told me. "I see your wheels churning, but I need you to talk to me."

I shifted in my chair. "I just have refined taste, Mrs. Polar," I finally said.

"I see," she replied. "And are you happy with how you acquire these finer things in life?"

I slightly arched the corner of my top lip. Mrs. Polar knew a bit about me, but she really didn't *know* me. She knew all the basics, but she had no idea that I'm a sugar baby. And my stepfather is one of my sugar daddies.

I know, here comes the judgement, the critics and their opinions. But it's truly not a bad gig. I don't sleep with all of my daddies, but I do sleep with a few. I don't sleep with my stepfather, but....

I focused on my therapist again. I rolled my eyes and let out a sigh as I began to answer her question.

"Once I graduate from school and land my dream job...or a job, there won't be a need for me to keep these people in my back pocket. They're my right-nows," I told her.

In reality, they were the main source of all my funding. I mean I had a part-time job to show face to my mom but......sorry Ma, ain't no job I can get at my age that pays *this* well. I can't wait to move out and live on campus. Then I could just be and answer to no one.

"I think you should take some alone time, Michelle. I know you said you have a family vacation this week. That could be the perfect setting to turn off your phone and spend quality time with your family. You said everyone would be in attendance, correct?"

I nodded.

"Great! This might be one of the last chances for you to have quality time with your folks before heading off to college in the fall. See it as an opportunity to connect with both your mom and stepfather. You said your brother was also coming from New York and I'm sure he'll be excited to catch up with you as well."

As if on cue, the beeping sound of the timer filled the

room. I stood up from the couch and grabbed my small yellow Balenciaga triangle duffle off the side table. Mrs. Polar met me at the door.

"See you in a week, Michelle. Have a wonderful vacation."

I exited the office space on Winter Street in Downtown Boston and waited for my Uber at Park Street Station. Kyle, my stepfather, sent me a ride so we could meet up. I wasn't sure what he wanted discuss, but we usually just had pretty quick 'touch and go' meetings. Kyle finding out about my hustle was a complete accident, but it has worked in both our favors.

I was on the website, Seeking Arrangement, and a photo-less profile hit me up. He said he was from the Boston area and after a few messages we agreed to meet at Capital Grille. I made sure to wear my tightest black dress and did an updo for my bundles.

As I strutted confidently to my awaiting table, my tantalizing eyes projected horror when I realized Kyle was waiting for me.

"Surprised to see me," he asked with his Spanish twang.

I looked around the room in shock, wondering if my mom was about to jump out and bust me for my illicit job choice.

"Yeah...what are you doing here? What's going on?" I said as I sat down.

"Well, Michelle...I'm sorry, I mean M. Lovely..." he started as I adjusted myself in my seat. "Let's cut straight to the chase. I like to take care of women. I want to take care of you if you let me."

I knew when ma left daddy things wouldn't be the same, but now here I am with this dickhead in front of me. Honestly – in that moment - to get back at ma, I didn't even mind entertaining Kyle, but I couldn't let him know I'd consider so quickly.

"And if I don't?" I snapped back.

He shrugged. "If you're not with it, cool. I won't pressure you...but I like you, Michelle," he finished.

I took a moment to think about the proposition. I scooted closer to him in my chair and leaned forward.

"Are you asking me for pussy, Kyle?" I said bluntly, my eyes squinted as I tried to decipher his end game.

"I don't need it," he said.

"So what *do* you need?" I was starting to get uncomfortable and he noticed.

He relaxed. "Honestly, Michelle, you don't have to fuck me. I can see where that could be a mindfuck for you and I'm not here to cause any trauma. But you're not ten years old anymore either, so you can tell me what's too much. In return I'll make sure you're well taken care of, always."

That was six months ago.

Kyle's needs were basic. He mainly wanted phone sex and I never understood why. I mean, wouldn't you want the real thing? I never got how a 35-year-old man could be so into listening to someone cum. Like that's all you're doing. Listening. Strange to me. Although this didn't faze me, I did worry that although he would just listen to me, he would be fucking someone not my mom.

I hopped in my Uber and headed toward destination unknown since Kyle had ordered the car. Guess the driver must be confident in his directions 'cause he didn't confirm with me the drop-off point.

I scanned my outfit through my shades. I was looking so cute today, courtesy of my daddies. My bundles were paid for by Jack, a chubby white daddy in D.C. My shiny off-the-shoulder velvet top by Elizabeth and James meshed well with my DL1961 white denim, which hugged me so right. I got the whole outfit with Bill's money from Texas. But of all I had on, it was the Roger Vivier buckle leather block heels that stole the show. That was Kyle's purchase.

I wondered what surprise he had in store today. He claimed he would buy away his guilt because he knew it was fucked up dealing with his wife's daughter but I didn't believe that.

I arrived at Legal's in the Seaport District at a quarter to four. I already knew where I was going in the restaurant so I didn't have to ask the hostess anything. In fact, I walked right by her, giving her a slight glare through my red and yellow Tapestry Prada's. Up the stairs, Kyle waited in the function room. I got to the top floor and opened the wooden door. Kyle sat facing the door, sitting at a table.

I was surprised that there was no food.

I took off my glasses and walked over.

"Hey, Kyle," I said with a smile as I walked toward him. He looked at me with a strange, bleak expression as if something was up.

"Stop," he said.

I did. Right in my tracks. Now I was definitely confused.

"What's going on?" I asked and that's when he stood up.

"I....I can't have this relationship with you anymore Michelle—"

I cut him off. "Excuse me?!"

He let out a deep sigh and did an arm gesture before walking toward the window overlooking the harbor.

"Hello?" I was getting frustrated. I mean, he dropped that bomb on me and just walked away?

"Yo, Kyle! What the fuck?"

"Look, I'll still help you with basic shit and school, but I can't with the whole nine yards anymore. It's no Bueno," he finished, throwing on his Honduran accent.

I shook my head in disbelief. My eyes began to water. Kyle was my favorite daddy, not only because of convenience but his pockets as a chief executive officer and business director of Gilette. They were deep, and to know I wouldn't have access to *that* level of comfort hurt me.

That's when he stepped closer, his facial expression soft. "I mean, you know...we can always renegotiate terms if you didn't want to me go," he said. "I just need more than the phone, you know?"

We stood in silence for a few minutes, then I took three deep breaths before storming out of the function room.

I slid my Prada's back on and ordered my Uber home to finalize my packing. That helped pep me back up, packing. Cancun was gonna be lit!

But I still couldn't believe Kyle just wasted my time like that...and made such a wild proposition.

Asshole.

****

Since we arrived in Cancun yesterday, Kyle and I haven't had two words to say to one another. But it's all good, cause I was doing the most to make him regret that choice.

As soon as we unpacked, I hit the dance floor looking fly and immediately started flirting with some 20-something dude. My mom and Kyle were nearby and I could feel Kyle staring, hard.

My poor 40-year-old mom had no clue what was going on with her man. And all I could do was shake my head. No, I didn't care because as far as I was concerned, she deserved every foul thing thrown her way. After all, she was the one who cheated on my real father with Kyle so the way I see it, karma's a bitch.

I had just returned to my room after letting the sun warm my melanin when I heard a knock on my door.

"Yeah?" I called out.

"Hey, Sis, it's me." I jumped up to let my big brother in.

"What's good, Jimmy? I'm gonna do a quick change for dinner..."

"Yeah but I wanted to ask you," he paused as he closed the door behind him, "what's up with K?"

Instantly my guard and nostrils went up. "The fuck? I dunno what's wrong with him," I said in a sharp tone.

"Yo chill," he said, pushing his palms down to get me to calm down. "I'm only asking cause, from the looks of things, he's been throwing drinks back since breakfast."

"Really?"

I knew Kyle used to drink a lot before he met my mom, and I had seen him order a drink at breakfast but I didn't think he was still going in at this hour. But then I shrugged it off and snapped out of it.

"I'm sure he's fine and just enjoying his vacation. Shit, I'm 'bout to do the same."

Jimmy nodded. "Yeah, you right, I'm probably just trippin'. A'ight, see you at the table."

After he left, I finished getting myself together and headed downstairs to the restaurant. Right away I spotted the family in the back corner.

I stepped confidently in my Fendi fun fair sandals toward the table. The sun illuminated my thighs and belly as I walked forward in my Supreme shorts and crop top for our 6PM dinner. A few tables stared, including my own. I noticed Kyle's glossy eyes and relaxed demeanor. Unfortunately, the only seat left at the table was next to him, so I sat.

For the most part, dinner was cool. Nice sea breeze coming in, good conversation with my mom and brother. But then I felt fingers on my thigh under the table cloth.

Someone was bold today.

I took my hand and swatted him away. But that wasn't enough. It went from fingers to his palm on my thigh. I shot him a look and sucked my teeth. He slowly moved his hand.

"What's wrong, Mish?" my mother asked, noticing my demeanor.

I rolled my eyes and sulked in my seat. "Nothing. I'm good," I said as I crossed my arms.

She gave me a 'if you say so look' and let it go. We sat for another 30 minutes, in which Kyle finished one drink and ordered another. Maybe his drinking had been excessive during the start of our family vacation, which probably explained his off behavior.

Like really, dude? Touching me at the table? While you're sitting next to my mother, your wife? If I didn't know better I'd say he was trying to get caught, but shit, don't drag me into it. My mom was foul and I wanted her to pay, but I didn't want her to know what I'd been doing.

Things were fairly calm as we finished up dinner. We all agreed we would go back to the club that night, so I went back to my room to shower and unwind before drinks with my bro.

I had just stepped out the bathroom with my towel when I

heard a knock at my door.

"Who is it?"

"Kyle..."

I paused for a second, almost deciding not to let him in. But finally, I swung the door open. "Uh....what's up Kyle?" I asked.

"I wanna talk about earlier..."

I stood for a minute, then said, fuck it. Maybe I could guilt him into sliding me a couple of coins.

"One sec," I said and closed back the door. I threw on my bra and panties and rewrapped my towel around me before reopening the door.

"Okay, what's up?"

"Can I come in?" he inquired.

"Nah, I'm good. What you wanna say?" I didn't want to give him much time.

"Hmm....well....you looked really nice earlier and I didn't know how to say it with everyone being there," he said.

"So you started rubbin' up on me? You've NEVER touched me before. Not cool, Kyle."

He stepped closer to me and I could smell the days' worth of liquor. "Mami, don't be like that..." he said.

I pulled my nose away and said, "I'll see you at the club" as I pushed him back and closed my door.

By the time Jimmy and I entered the club, the dance floor was packed. I was also pretty tipsy and was feeling myself. Eighteen was legal drinking age in Cancun so I was taking full advantage of it.

We were just turning up, doing Jolly Rancher shots and body shots. I was just about to get off the bar when I saw Kyle coming toward me. Last I'd seen, he was dancing with my mother on the opposite side of the club. He must've left my mom over there because he was alone now. When my feet touched the ground, Kyle stood in front of me.

"Hey, party girl!" He was slurring and stone-cold drunk. "Let me get a dance?"

I smirked. "Noooooooooooo thank you."

His face changed and turned serious. He grabbed my arm and tried to pull me onto the dance floor. Luckily, Jimmy grabbed me and Kyle realized he had to let me go cause of the resistance.

When Jimmy went to step to him, Kyle backed off and threw his arms up, dissolving into the crowd. I turned to Jimmy and explained I didn't know what his problem was.

The whole scene had shaken me and I kept my eye on Kyle across the club. A couple of hours had passed when I realized that I hadn't seen my mother. Kyle was chatting it up with some girl slightly older than me and I got annoyed. Jimmy noticed, too, but just shook his head. Jimmy never liked Kyle anyway and I was sure he liked him even less after this.

At three a-m, the lights came on and the club was emptied. I was fucked up. I'm talking lean-walk with giggles accompanying all the way. I wanted to keep the party going but Jimmy was saying it was time to turn down. Whatever.

I made it to the lobby and realized I had to piss something terrible. "Wait Jimmy, let me go to the bathroom first before we head upstairs!" I slurred.

While using my body to open the bathroom door, I noticed mom walk over from the elevators with an uneasy look on her face. As the door closed behind me I heard her say, "Jimmy, have you seen Kyle?"

I stumbled into my stall and began to piss when I heard

someone having sex a few doors down. Intrigued, I got on the floor to peak and see if I could see anything and boy did I see something.

Bouncing up and down was the chick from the club who Kyle had been posted up with all night.

"Oh, fuck no," I yelled and made my way to the last stall. I opened up the handicapped stall to see Kyle pull out of this chick, raw. "Are you serious, right now? Because you couldn't fuck me, you do this?" I yelled with deep pain in my voice. I don't know why seeing that hurt me so. It couldn't be because of my mom. And I had turned Kyle down. But for some reason, I was furious.

I turned to spin around and stomp out of the bathroom, only to come face to face with my mother.

I couldn't control my anger. All my pain came boiling to the surface. "Why did you have to cheat on daddy? Was it worth it? Was it all worth it?…"

The End

TL Jackson *is a writer and lover of urban reads and erotica from the Boston area, currently living in Hamilton, ON Canada. When she's not writing something steamy she's a content creator on other platforms.* www.tljacksonx.com *@tljacksonx — Instagram.*

13

UNDERNEATH

MY SKIN

By Patricia A. Bridewell

Las Vegas 2017

Where is she? Lena Stephens checked her watch for the umpteenth time while waiting for her best friend, Noreen. Honestly, they could've postponed this last-minute dinner celebration. The end of a bitter two-year divorce was nothing she cared to celebrate. In fact, it was an agonizing reminder of a day she longed to forget.

As she waited, her mind raced back to the day Sherman asked for a divorce, the day her whole world stopped.

"Babe, I love you, but... I'm sorry. You don't excite me

anymore and I want a divorce."

Lena gasped and clutched her chest. For a moment she couldn't speak, move, or breath. Lifting a Shona Stone bust from the dining room table, she raised her arms to make the pitch but froze. Did she want to die or go to jail? Lena placed the bust back on the table and cried.

In hindsight, she should've clobbered him and knocked some sense into his head. Or had her own head examined. Instead, Lena lived in denial, refuting Sherman's alleged affair with a younger woman. Her friends were all liars. Troublemakers. Miserable people who wanted to destroy her marriage. What a fool!

Noreen's loud mouth broke her reverie.

"Woot, Woot!Congratulations!" Noreen shouted as she strolled into Lawry's Prime Rib, holding a cake box. She placed a coconut cake and a manila envelope in front of Lena and hugged her.

"You're late. Who's the cake for?"

"You. I stopped by the bakery. Open the envelope. You're officially a single woman now."

Lena stared at the envelope and said, "Thanks, but we didn't have to meet for this." The last thing on her mind was divorce, cake, or food. She needed a personal trainer - someone who could motivate her to set goals for healthier living, the first step of her beauty transition.

"That's what real friends do. Girl, you've been through a lot." Noreen slid into the seat across from her. "You should want to see, hold, smell that piece of paper."

They laughed, though Lena's laugh was marred with painful undertones. Noreen summoned the waiter to their table and ordered drinks.

Noreen wasn't just her friend and divorce attorney, she and her husband, Rob, were Lena's business partners. They'd managed their Divorce and Family Law Practice for over two decades and handled most of the legwork on the business plan for Lena's medical supplies company.

The waiter brought two glasses of wine and salads.

"Guess what? I got my first surgery date," Lena said, watching Noreen's reaction.

"I thought you said you'd wait." Noreen tapped a message on her cell.

"Can't wait. I have to be fine before our Grand Opening." She picked up a cup of low-calorie Italian Dressing and poured it over her salad.

Noreen glanced over her glasses. "Think about this. Your chance is now. What's more important? Plastic surgery or a business?"

"Both. I'm ecstatic about the business," Lena said, sighing. "But I want to feel the same way about myself."

"Hon, that'll change after the business opens," Noreen said, sticking a fork in her salad. "Why not try Botox or wrinkle cream? Anything instead of going under the hatchet. Surgeries have risks, you know?"

Lena shook her head and pointed thumbs down. "Botox injections are out. Wrinkle cream is out. I have no confidence in all the hype on T.V. I'm having surgery."

Despite some differences in opinions, Lena respected her friend's honesty and blunt rhetoric. Even though she had no clue about single life in 2017.

"I get your point. Just don't understand the surgery. I mean, you look great." Wagging her fork at Lena, Noreen asked, "What're you having done?"

Lena didn't respond, but the expression on her friend's face made her think twice about concealing her secret.

"Okay, okay, don't judge me. I'm having a full body makeover and a facelift." She held up a palm. "Not all at once."

Noreen frowned. "Have you lost your mind? You talk to Ashley about this?"

Lena gave a dismissive hand wave. "I'm in my right mind, and Ashley knows." Lena smiled and added, "Besides, I think that daughter of mine is falling in love. Someday, I will, too."

Noreen sipped her wine, leaned over the table and whispered, "Not if you don't start dating. Black folks don't get all that surgery."

"Well, some do. A co-worker of mine had a facelift last year. Worked wonders for her! Now she's dating men in the millennial range."

"Who cares? You want to date a toddler or a mature man?"

"I'd like to date. Period. Eventually, anyway."

She studied her friend's face. Not a wrinkle in sight. Much younger than Lena and nearing her mid-fifties, Noreen was still a bombshell so she couldn't possibly understand. It was painful to accept her friend's opinions, but that wouldn't derail Lena's decision.

"Let's say you get the surgery. And you're super fine, like a Tyra Banks look-a-like," Noreen said, twirling her hand. "Will you tell men your real age?"

Lena's eyes narrowed, and she said, "No. That's for me to know, and for you to keep a secret."

Beverly Hills, CA 2018

That was then; today is now.

Once Lena set foot in the Montage Hotel – Beverly Hills, chit-chat dwindled among the well-dressed black businessmen in the lobby. Mr. Gray Suit, who wore a Fedora, caught her gaze and didn't shift his center of attention.

"Good afternoon, welcome to the Montage Hotel – Beverly Hills. May I help you?" the hotel clerk asked.

"Yes, I'm Lena Stephens, my reservation is for three nights. Dunson and Lattimore Conference." She handed the clerk her driver's license and American Express, then peered over at Mr. Gray Suit's clean-shaven amber brown face. Handsome. He winked and tipped his Fedora; she flashed a smile and turned back to the clerk.

"Can the bellhop bring my luggage upstairs?"

"Sure." The clerk handed back her information and two keycards. "You're in Room 1243. Enjoy your stay."

"My pleasure." Lena sashayed down the hallway, confident that her red-cellophaned bob was intact. Wearing a navy-blue suit and pearls, her black Louboutin's clicked the polished floors as she journeyed toward the elevator. Midway, she heard footsteps and spun around to Mr. Gray Suit. Mercy!

"Hopefully, I didn't scare you." He extended his hand and said, "I'm Kyle. May I ask your name?"

She smiled and grasped his hand. "Lena, and no you didn't."

"Please forgive me for shadowing you. You're stunning. Are you here for an event?"

Lena tilted her head. "Maybe. Did you guess or rub a crystal ball?"

Kyle chuckled and swiped his chin. "Ahh, A woman with a sense of humor. I guessed. Haven't seen many black women here."

The elevator chimed; large steel doors divided.

"Excuse me. Nice meeting you." She brushed past him and entered the elevator.

He quickly reached inside his jacket for a business card and handed it to her. "Call me about cocktails and dinner this evening," he said before the elevator doors closed.

Lena stuffed the card inside her purse and rolled her eyes. She'd tossed out many cards, most from businessmen on the prowl. *He's probably another executive playboy with a wife and babies at home.* After re-entering the dating world, she'd learned the hard way to trust no one until they'd earned it.

She exited the elevator, tipped the bellhop, then strolled through the room, viewing a king-sized bed, Cherrywood desk, and a caramel-colored velvet chaise lounge sofa. After kicking off her heels and undressing, Lena gazed in a full-length mirror, still amazed with her well-toned body. All the liposuction, snips, and tucks were worth the time and labor involved. And the facelift... A vast transformation from Madea to a Black Cinderella.

And Noreen said she shouldn't have surgery.

Cleaning her face, she gazed at her satin brown skin. Wrinkle-free. Passing for a woman in her mid-thirties was a cinch, yet underneath the layers, she knew the truth. In two years, she'd celebrate seventy years on this planet, and she'd have her own Prince Harry before then.

****

Now, where are those sunglasses? Lena hadn't realized her sunglasses were missing until hours later. She'd searched the room multiple times to no avail, dropped to her knees and checked under the bed. No luck. She'd have to go downstairs, so she slipped on a lavender sweat suit, Nike tennis, and applied lipstick.

Walking into the lobby, she noticed the clerk holding up her red eyeglass case. "I thought you'd come back. So, I waited."

"I appreciate that," Lena said, accepting the case.

She strolled to the elevator but paused when she saw Kyle entering the Gift Shop. Lena put on the sunglasses—ducked her head and sprinted in another direction to avoid him. He was cute, but she hadn't planned on getting cushy with a man she'd just met in the hotel lobby. Plus, she wasn't wearing any makeup, and had on a sweat suit, too?

"Lena!" Kyle yelled, jogging to catch up.

Her lips puckered before she slid on a smile and twirled around. "Oh, we meet again."

"Are you rushing out? I was hoping we'd have dinner and drinks, but you didn't call."

"No. I uh...I'm not sure about dinner." She stuck both hands inside her sweat suit jacket. "I have to finish some work." She lied, but what else could she say?

"Me, too. A ton of work. My proposition is limit dinner to say...two hours. Is that okay?" he asked in a gentle voice.

His pleasant-smelling cologne swirled around her head, and those denim jeans and a black polo shirt fit his chiseled physique perfectly. She'd be crazy to decline his offer.

"We don't have to leave the hotel," he said with raised brows. The Rooftop Grill has great food and a view of the city.

"I've heard of that restaurant," she said, refocusing on his question. "I'd love to go there."

Kyle lifted an elbow. "Come on. You're in for a treat." She looped her arm through his, and their date began.

From the time they exited the elevator, she became more comfortable. Cozy atmosphere. The Rooftop Grill was literally on the roof, had no walls, but decorative stainless-steel dividers. A roof covered part of the restaurant. Adjacent was the outside patio with a pool, extra tables, and a scenic view of the city. Glass-top tables with tall vases of multi-colored flowers lit up the environment.

Kyle asked for outside seating and ordered drinks, then reached for Lena's hand, and they walked to the ledge for a better view.

"What's your first impression?" he asked.

"Breathtaking. This view is amazing."

Kyle wrapped his arm around Lena's shoulder; they gazed deeply into one another's eyes, and then at the blue sky, hillside homes on the slopes of Hollywood Hills, and a section of downtown L.A.

When the waiter returned with their drinks, they went back to the table and ordered dinner — salmon for Lena; Kyle ordered shrimp and salad. He folded his hands on the table and watched her intently, which caused some discomfort. But when their eyes locked, she sensed it wouldn't take long to adjust to his warm brown eyes.

"Time flies. Do you mind if we cut out business talk?"

"Not at all," Lena said. *A businessman who doesn't want to discuss business?*

"First, tell me about you." he said.

She shrugged. "Born and raised in L.A. I have a BA and MBA, love to travel when I can. I'm divorced, no children, and I live here in L.A." *Dang! I hate lying about Ashley. What the* heck could I do? I'm passing for thirty-six. I sure can't tell this man about my thirty-two-year-old daughter. She fumbled with her charm bracelet.

"Hmm…Impressive. I travel due to my work, but my home base is here, too. Where'd you go to school?"

"Cal-State L.A. and Pepperdine. Before I go on, tell me more about you," Lena said.

"Single, almost married, no babies' daddy issues." He laughed and lifted a finger. "I'm a proud father to my nephew, though. I've had him since he was twelve."

"What an awesome act of love. How old is he now?"

"Oh, he just made seventeen, and will be off to college next year. And by the way, I went to college, too. Fisk University."

"Fisk? That's great."

"Are you dating or in a serious relationship?" Kyle asked.

"Not at the moment," Lena said with a smile. "Are you?"

"No," he said, shaking his head. "Believe me if I had a woman, I wouldn't be so enchanted with you."

"Whoa. Enchanted?" Lena said, placing a palm to her chest. You just met me."

"True. When you walked in the hotel, I couldn't take my eyes off you. I want to know you better."

Although Lena was ambivalent about Kyle disclosing his feelings this soon, she couldn't deny her instant attraction after she noticed him in the lobby this morning.

"I'd like to know more about you, too. You said your job requires traveling. Did your job get in the way of marriage and a family?"

"Yes. A few years ago, my mindset was strictly on making money. Now I'm ready to settle down with the right woman," he said keeping his eyes on Lena.

"Lena. Is that you?" A familiar voice interrupted their conversation from afar. When she stood to find the voice, her shoulders slumped. Cynthia Rigby. Why is she in L.A.? Cynthia scurried to the table with a briefcase over her shoulder.

"I thought I saw you earlier. What are you doing down here?" Cynthia asked, eyeing her up and down.

"I'm here for a conference."

"Changed your hair color, I see. It's beautiful." They hugged. "How do you keep that figure? You look different?"

"Uh, this is Kyle. Cynthia was my realtor," Lena said, ignoring her question.

"Hi, Cynthia Rigby." She handed him a business card and pulled out a chair next to his. "I sell residential property in Nevada. There's a lot of reasonable property out there."

Lena's spirit sank with the idea that Cynthia may be planning to eat with them. She forced a smile to hide her dismay.

Kyle read the card. "I've heard." He lifted his head and glanced at Cynthia. "I may call you. Had thoughts of checking out properties in Vegas. So, are you here on business or vacation?"

"Our Realtors Association Conference ended today." Staring at Kyle, she rested her chin on clasped hands. "If you've got a family, I have a new four-bedroom home in Henderson."

Lena let out a long breath she'd been holding in. It was past time for Cynthia to skedaddle. But no-o-o, she's bogarting my date.

"No. It's just me and my seventeen-year-old nephew."

Cynthia looked at Lena. "You still have the house I sold

you in Henderson?"

Kyle's brows raised; his gaze shifted to Lena, then he picked up his cell and started texting.

"No, I sold it after my divorce. I moved back here this year and I have a medical supplies business now." What was she thinking? Asking all those personal questions in front of Kyle.

"Really? After all those years?" Cynthia said, frowning. And your daughter, Asia. Is she at home or married?"

I'm doomed. "Ashley. She's my niece and single."

Busybody Cynthia's questions had jumped high on the Richter Scale, and Lena was pissed. Afraid that she'd keep yakking and bring up facts that would reveal her actual age, Lena picked up her cell and got up. "Cynthia, give me your number so we can catch up."

"Of course. Sorry. I've been running my mouth." Her eyes wandered back to Kyle.

"Listen, I'm going to the Ladies Room. Walk with me, and we'll exchange numbers," Lena said. "Kyle, I'll be back shortly."

"Whenever you're in Nevada, give me a ring," Cynthia said, smiling and batting her fake eyelashes as they walked away. Lena cut her eyes. This woman had crossed the line of professionalism. Yes, Kyle was a sweet piece of candy, but for all she knew, he could've been hers.

Lena returned and sat across from Kyle. "Sorry about that." She rubbed her hands together as the waiter lifted steaming plates from the tray and set them on the table. Kyle appeared surprised by her comment.

"You mean Cynthia?"

Lena nodded.

"She wasn't a problem for me. Her sales pitch was together,

minus the flirting," he said, rubbing the side of his face and looking at Lena.

Her eyes roamed to his; she grinned. "I guess you're right." They both laughed, and that eased Lena's tension.

"Did she mention you had a daughter in Nevada?"

Almost choking on the water she'd swallowed, Lena coughed and cleared her throat.

"You okay?"

She raised a hand. "She meant Ashley, my niece. I've always called her my daughter. My ex-husband and I lived in Henderson, and she stayed with us for several years."

"Mmm...okay, I missed that part. How is she doing now?"

"She's fine," Lena said, cutting her salmon. Completing her first year at Columbia University in New York. Honor student, well-adjusted." Well, she did go to Columbia...ten years ago.

"Ivy League...that's excellent. Oh, I got a text. I have a meeting after dinner. How long will you be at the hotel?"

"For three days. After the conference, I have another meeting the next day and it's close by. So, I booked a room to avoid driving in traffic. I opened a medical supply company, and I'm seeking new distributors.

"Really? I do imports and exports and have connections in that business. Let's chat about that one day." Kyle leaned forward and said, "I'd really like to see you again."

Lena wanted to say 'yes' but she desired a committed relationship and marriage. Most of the men she'd dated claimed to have a devout interest in marriage. They lied. Would Kyle? but was skeptical. That scene with Cynthia was bothersome. Several things about him held her attention, but above all his genuine personality and being a father figure to his nephew were number one.

Kyle crisscrossed his hands to get her attention. "Is that a yea or nay?"

"Why not?" Lena said, laughing.

Dating him may be risky, but she'd take a chance. They ate and kept their agreement, sharing only personal interests. At 5:50 p.m., Kyle rushed out for his meeting. Lena ordered another glass of wine and walked back to the ledge where she and Kyle stood earlier, unable to erase him from her mind. What if they fell in love? Could she tell him the truth about her age if their relationship became serious?

Suddenly, her thoughts went to pause. They hadn't exchanged information. Then she remembered that she had his business card.

****

The cell phone woke Lena from a half-dazed sleep. Too much wine last night. She rolled over and picked up the phone.

"Hello."

"Good morning, Mom."

Lena pried her tired eyes open and sat straight up in bed. Yawning, she said, "Ashley, baby. How are you?"

"I'm engaged, that's how I am," she said, giggling.

Lena threw her head back. "Oh, my gosh. When did this happen?"

"Mom, calm down. Ethan proposed last night."

"Ethan?" She swung her feet to the floor, uttering 'my prayer is answered' under her breath. She was thrilled to know Ethan had proposed. He had an excellent job and treated Ashley like a queen.

"Mom, can you speak louder? I didn't hear what you said."

"Congratulations! When is the wedding?"

"We don't know yet, but we'll be in L.A. soon. I'm at work so I gotta go. Just wanted to tell you that. Love you."

"Love you, too. Honey, call me Sunday." For a few minutes, Lena couldn't move. She was too emotional. Her thirty-two year old baby girl lived in Dallas, but their busy schedules hadn't prevented them from staying in touch by texting, Face-Time, or phone.

On her way to the conference, Lena wondered how she and Kyle would meet each other since she couldn't find his business card. She arrived precisely at 7:30 a.m. for the breakfast and networking, and they dismissed for a one-hour lunch at 11:45. Kyle exited from another door of the conference room, talking with two other men.

When he noticed Lena, he whispered to one of the men, then walked her way.

"Hello, there," he said with a toothy grin.

"Hi. I didn't know you were attending this conference."

He nodded and said, "Yes, I am. Before I forget again, can I get your number?"

"Good suggestion. It's 323-297-4780. Lena Stephens is my full name."

He typed it in. "Do you have my number?"

"I misplaced your card."

"No worries," he said, seemingly in a hurry. He dialed Lena's phone; she answered. "Now you have mine. My last name's Wilson. Here's the deal. I had planned lunch for us, but something came up. I wanted to call you last night about lunch today. I didn't have your number, and now something's come up. What about dinner this evening? I'm leaving town tomorrow morning."

"Two or three weeks? Lena asked, frowning. "I don't know what I'll be doing. "You're not staying for the full conference?"

He touched her shoulder. "I know that seems odd, but I need to fly out to Taiwan. I'm leaving town tomorrow."

"Well, Yes, let's go to dinner."

"That's great. I'll text you around 5:45."

"The conference ends at 3:00, so I'll be ready."

He lifted and kissed the back of her hand. Motionless, after his soft lips touched her hand, she shuddered. Kyle seemed debonair and sincere, but his job involved traveling, and that might create problems. She questioned whether a relationship with him would grow or fizzle in time.

When she returned to the conference after lunch, Kyle was gone, but she observed the two men from earlier. She introduced herself to the sales representatives from the Dunson and Lattimore Medical Supplies and Distribution Company. They welcomed her with brochures and accepted her business card, which left Lena optimistic for a future relationship with this renowned company. Finding a major medical supply distributor was crucial since her new company's sales had soared.

****

Glancing in the mirror, Lena applied a coat of red lipstick, and pressed powder to her face. She picked up her phone to check the text message tone. It was from Kyle. He'd drive in front of the hotel in five minutes.

Kyle picked Lena up, drove to Marina del Rey and parked in the restaurant's lot.

"Our reservation is at 7:00 so we have time to chat. Thank

you for accepting my dinner invitation," Kyle said, in a serious tone.

"No problem. I enjoyed last night. What time is your flight to Taiwan?"

"Seven-fifteen tomorrow morning, and too early, he said, shaking his head. I'd hoped we could get together tomorrow before I leave the country. That's not possible because I had to change my flight time."

"Wait a minute, Lena said, lifting a hand and laughing. Another date? "Aren't you on a roll with this dating matter."

Kyle glanced at Lena and placed his hand over hers. "I'd say so. Lady, I'm attracted to you."

"I'm glad to hear that. I feel the same. Let's…you know," she shrugged, "take it a step at a time."

"I'm okay with that. Believe me, I plan to win your heart. Now tell me something about your company and the things you like to do for enjoyment."

Lena and Kyle talked for over an hour, and their conversation continued over a plate of crab legs, baked potatoes, and asparagus with glasses of wine. The night was intriguing, they discussed the places where they'd traveled, their hobbies, families, and more. Kyle was a gentleman and she loved that. One issue bothered Lena. He didn't disclose much about his business and that was strange.

****

Over a month had passed, and although their third dinner date was cancelled, Kyle had kept his promise and called. What surprised her most was he'd called two, sometimes three times a week from various locations. He'd called from Taiwan,

Houston, San Francisco, and Washington, D.C. Tonight, she was excited that she'd get to see him again.

As always, she dialed Noreen whenever she was going out with someone new.

"Hey," Noreen said.

"I'll be leaving soon."

"Okay, one thing. Did you get the name of Kyle's business?"

"No, I didn't. He'll eventually tell me."

"Well, like I said, we still have crooks in this world. I couldn't find a Kyle Wilson in imports and exports. Try to get his birth date and place of birth."

"Girl, stop! I'm not asking him that information," Lena said, pushing a hand to her hip.

"Lena, I need it."

"No, because then he'll want mine."

"So, what? He'll ask your age one day. Find out who Kyle Wilson really is."

Why'd she have to go there with the age madness? Noreen was cautious, and she appreciated her concerns. But doing a background check on the man?

"Gotcha! Text you when I get back."

Kyle texted that he was out front; she set her house alarm and strolled down the driveway. Holding his cell, Lena noticed him talking until he saw her walking toward the truck. The gleam on his face, the way his lips parted as she approached the tan Range Rover, lifted her spirit. He hopped out of the car with a red rose in hand and opened the passenger side.

"Lady, you're absolutely beautiful," he said. Handing her the rose, he pulled Lena closer and pecked her cheek, and they kissed passionately, which nearly lifted her from the ground.

"This rose is beautiful," she said, studying his strong jawline and short hair.

He gazed into her eyes and said, "I've missed you."

"After they got in the truck, he looked at Lena. "We need to talk. If you don't mind, dinner will be at my beach house."

Lena squinted. "Really? Where's your house?"

"In Malibu. If you object, maybe we can do it here."

"No, I'm fine with your place," she said, with splayed fingers. Knowing full well she wasn't. Thoughts about Noreen's warning when dating new men came to mind, she thought about requesting they go to a restaurant. She hadn't noticed any red flags, so she dismissed those thoughts.

When he drove up to a gorgeous Malibu home and double-car garage, Lena felt a little uncomfortable again. They walked upstairs, and he gave her a tour of the spacious three-bedroom, tri-level home. He ordered Chinese food, and they sat on the deck, ate, and listened to jazz. It was eighty degrees outside and the sun and sea breeze against her skin was relaxing.

Lena searched Kyle's face before she spoke. "What did you want to talk about?"

"Uncle Kyle, I didn't know you'd be here," a man said, stepping outside.

"Uh, Terrence, same here. This is Lena."

Lena's back to Terrence, she twirled around to speak. Her mouth opened, but the words stuck in her throat.

"Ms. Lena?" he said, smiling. "Wow, are you two dating?"

No, this couldn't be happening. Not today, tomorrow, or ever.

"What's wrong," Kyle asked, placing his arm around her shoulder. She jerked away and jumped to her feet. "I have to go. Now!"

"Wait, let's talk. Sweetheart, are you okay?" Kyle asked.

She barged through the open glass door and grabbed her purse from the kitchen table. Pausing, she didn't remember how to exit, so she rushed to the nearest door with Kyle on her heels.

"Where are you going? Remember, you didn't drive," he said, flinging his arms.

Slightly out of breath, she stopped at the door, too embarrassed to face Kyle. She gazed at the floor. He stepped up from behind and placed both hands on her shoulders then whispered softly in her ear, "Talk to me."

"I don't know if I can," she said, covering her mouth.

"Why don't you try?"

With her back to him, she said, "Talk to Terrence first. I'll wait on the deck."

"But what does Terr—"

"Just do it," she said, cutting him off. "We can talk afterward. If not, please take me home."

Lena waited until she heard Kyle's footsteps fade in the hallway before she moved. Why did she think this would work? She mustered up energy to trek out to the deck, watching the ocean, taking deep breaths, wondering. It seemed like an eternity before he returned.

Kyle appeared weary when he exited with two bottles of Perrier. He handed Lena one bottle and opened his bottle.

"Well. Who talks first? You or me?" he asked.

With a bowed head, Lena said, "I will. I'm so sorry. It wasn't my intent to deceive or hurt you. After thirty-three years of marriage, my husband left me for a younger woman. That hurt and humiliated me. She explained how plastic surgery had boosted her self-esteem and helped her move forward.

"And…Ashley is my daughter. She's thirty-two, not eighteen."

"I understand," Kyle said, crossing his legs. "I know I haven't been transparent. I brought you here to talk about the things you should know about me. I never married but came close. My former girlfriend of eleven years packed and left one day. She wanted marriage and kids, I was too wrapped up in my business." He confessed their breakup devastated him, and at that time he was older and lonely.

"I was unhappy with aging and had two facelifts done years ago."

"Really?" Lena asked.

"Yes, so, there you have it. Terrence Ethan Lattimore goes by his middle name, and he is thirty-three. After my sister passed away, I raised him. Both of his parents are deceased, and he kept me busy." Kyle chewed his bottom lip and said, "One last thing. I'm Kyle Dunson. And I'll admit, I overheard your name when you checked in at the Montage. Then I found out you had registered for our conference. So, you'll get a call from one of my Sales team regarding a distribution contract."

Lena lifted her head. "Why didn't you tell me who you were?"

"For the same reason you told me Ashley was your niece and eighteen. This is nuts…but from the time I saw you at the Montage, I knew I had to go after you."

"Yep, you did just that. All the way to the elevator." Lena laughed.

"Right, and I feared you'd learn the truth."

"I can't believe how much I lied. I was scared stiff that you'd find out the truth about me, too," Lena said taking sips of water.

"Lesson learned, it's not what's on the outside that counts," Kyle said.

"Where do we go from here?" Lena asked, clasping her hands." Hoping, quietly praying he would not end their relationship. Would he trust her; could she trust him?

Kyle placed his hand on top of hers. "I believe this whole situation revolved around one person who'd lost love, another who'd never accepted it. In my heart, I think we're meant for each other.

"I do, too. Can we start all over?" Lena asked.

"Yes, no more lies or secrets," Kyle said, rising and kissing her cheek. Give me a minute."

Lena laughed when she heard the Four Tops song "Ain't No Woman Like the One I Got."

Kyle came out and reached for Lena's hand. "May I have this dance?"

Lena held his hand as she got up. He wrapped his arms around her waist; she closed her eyes and leaned against his chest. She opened her eyes and said, "Wait! Can we fall in love? Ethan and Ashley are getting married."

Kyle laughed. "It's too late to ask. You keep tugging at my heart strings, there might be another engagement real soon."

The End

Patricia A. Bridewell's love for reading transitioned to pen and paper in 2007. She writes Inspirational Romance and Women's Fiction. Visit her on social media and www.patriciabridewell.com.

14

VIEWER DISCRETION IS ADVISED

By Latasha Holloway

"Clear!" yelled the production manager in the Channel 5 news studio.

Andrea Jones, the co-anchor for the five o'clock news at WTVF - Nashville, hopped off the chair at the desk. She had a fifteen minute break before she'd have to return to the set.

"Can you take off my mic so I can go into my dressing room for a few minutes?" Andrea asked the sound assistant. She needed to take a break because she'd have to keep it together for the next segment. It was a hard story that had been running for about two weeks.

There was a serial killer in the city and it was getting harder to cover the story because the murders of Nashville therapists were increasing and becoming more gruesome.

Inside her dressing room, Andrea looked at her reflection in the floor length mirror. She needed a few touch-ups and she'd do that herself. The station's makeup artist never touched her mocha skin; she didn't allow it because of how past artists never used the correct foundation or colors to make her skin glow on camera.

Once she handled her makeup, she stood again in front of the mirror. "You can do this. You are smart, sexy and fierce!"

This was her usual pep talk before going on every evening. She rubbed her hands down her dress, looking at her petite five-foot-nothing frame, but when she glanced into the mirror again, she heard the voice.

You're lying! You wrote those letters! You just want attention! I'm going to give you all the attention that want.

Tears sprang to her eyes and she cowered against the wall to block the blows she knew were coming. But then, she closed her eyes and shook her head to rid the memory.

"Pull it together, girl," she whispered to herself.

The knock on the door brought her back to the present.

"Andrea, on set. Five minutes."

Taking a few deep breaths, she straightened her clothes, careful to keep her eyes away from the mirror before she left her dressing room.

****

"Today, another therapist was found dead in his office. Police believe he is the fourth victim of the Nashville serial killer. We go now to Stencil Page, who is live at the scene in

Carothers Park Shoppes in Franklin. Stencil, can you tell us what the police are saying?"

The camera cut to the office location and the reporter. "Thanks, Andrea. Police think it may have been one of the therapist's patients."

As the reporter continued, Andrea shuffled the papers in front of her.

The reporter said, "There isn't forced entry and the office was not in disarray, except for the body of Dr. Nathaniel O'Neal. We were allowed to see the office from the door where the murder took place. The video we're about to show is not for the weak at heart. We've blurred out most of it, but viewer discretion is advised."

The video played across the screen, showing the blurred dismembered body of the doctor and the profanity that was written on the wall in the doctor's blood.

"Stencil, can you tell us if the police have any suspects in custody?" Andrea asked.

"They don't at this time, but they do believe that this murder is linked to the other cases of the murdered therapists."

"Do they still believe that the killer is a female?"

"When I spoke with the lead detective on the case, Detective Thomas said that they are moving away from that theory now as the last few victims were dismembered. Like the last time, Dr. O'Neal's index finger and penis were severed. We will have more from the scene this evening. Live from Franklin, this is Stencil Page reporting."

"Thank you, Stencil." Andrea looked into the camera.

"We will be back with different ideas to celebrate the fourth of July after this commercial break."

A beat and then, "Clear!"

****

Andre Jones walked into Dr. Irwin Jacobs's office for his nightly appointment. He'd been meeting with the doctor for the last week and felt like they were making good progress helping him to deal with his abusive past. Andre was just happy the doctor had been willing to meet with him after hours to accommodate his schedule.

"Hi, Andre," Dr. Jacob greeted him. "You're right on time." He motioned for Andre to have a seat.

Dr. Jacob's office was set up like the many other therapist's offices he'd visited: There was the couch and two arm chairs with a coffee table in between.

As always, Andre didn't offer a greeting; he just walked in and sat on the right side of the sofa as usual.

Dr. Jacobs said, "I was hoping we could break the pattern tonight and just jump right into session. Is that okay with you?" The doctor sat behind his desk instead of sitting in the chair close to Andre the way he usually did. This was going to be his last night session. Having heard about his friend and colleague being murdered, he knew he needed to be more cautious and not be in the office too late.

When he didn't hear a response, the doctor looked up and was startled a bit to find Andre no longer sitting but standing close to the desk. The look on his face was not one Dr. Jacob recognized. It was an emotion he wanted to delve into. "What has you looking so hurt right now?"

"Why are you sitting over here tonight?"

"I thought we should try something different. You've been taking some time to warm up when you first arrive and maybe it's because you're a little uncomfortable with the close proximity."

Andre evaluated Dr. Jacobs's words, but there was something different about his demeanor. He shrugged, then returned to the couch. "Okay, let's get this going. I have somewhere to be."

"That's what I like to hear. Where are we going to start tonight?" Dr. Jacobs pulled out the digital voice recorder and pressed record.

"I've been trying to deal with possibly losing my mom. She's been sick for the past month and the doctors haven't been able to find out why she's losing weight." Andre swiped his hand across his beard; he was on the verge of tears.

"I'm sorry to hear that about your mom, but let's talk about the abuse by your father." Dr. Jacobs glanced down at his notes. "That's where we left off our last session."

"Why did you ask me where we're going to start if you were going to direct the conversation anyway?" Andre shouted, his deep baritone voice resonating through the room. "What if I don't want to talk about my father tonight?" He suddenly stood up, flipping the coffee table in the process.

Dr. Jacobs didn't flinch. "Does it make you angry to change the direction of the conversation away from your mom's illness?" He motioned toward the sofa. "Have a seat and we … I mean, please have a seat so we can continue the conversation."

Dr. Jacobs wasn't concerned. He was sure the rage was fake and could barely contain his laughter. Andre was only five feet and had a very slim build that reminded him more of a woman than a man.

Andre stood staring, refusing to answer Dr. Jacobs's

question. There was malice in his eyes, but all Dr. Jacobs did was recline a bit in his chair as if he was waiting for Andre's anger to pass.

Andre paused, his anger on full display, then turned and walked out of the office.

"Andre!"

He ignored Dr. Jacobs calling his name.

****

"Hey, aren't you Andrea Jones from Channel Five news?"

Andrea turned to look at the guy standing behind her in line in the *Icon in the Gulch* coffee bar. She gave a brilliant smile and nodded.

"Oh my God, you are so fine! I am such a big fan! Can I have your autograph?"

His voice made everyone in the coffee bar stop and stare.

One of the patrons, sitting at a table who'd been working on his computer, heard her name and looked up. Andrea Jones? Her name was almost the same as his. He leaned over a bit to get a good look at her and his eyes widened. *She looks like my twin. We're the same height, the same build, the same complexion.*

He stood and moved toward the crowd gathering around Andrea. When he had a chance, he reached out his hand to her. "Hi, I'm Andre Jones."

Andrea looked up into eyes that were the same light brown color of hers. A shocked expression crossed her face.

The crowd around them responded the same way. Everyone quieted, surprised at the resemblance.

Andrea was the first to speak. "You have my face... well sort of and eyes. W-Who? W-What?" Her expression was filled with confusion.

They stood staring at each other and the crowd remained in place staring at them. Only the sound of the door opening broke the trance.

Andre asked, "Can we talk over there away from the crowd?"

"Yes. Let's sit down." With her drink in her hand, Andrea followed him and they began to talk: their ages — they were the same. Their family life — they were both only children, raised in abusive households. They had so much in common.

"I can't believe your father was abusive to you, too," Andrea said.

Andre nodded. "Yes, but he died when I was fifteen." His tone was sad, but inside he smiled. "What about your father? Is he still alive?"

"No, he died when I was fifteen, too. Our names and lives are too similar; don't you find that odd?"

Andre didn't answer at first, he was so deep into his thoughts. Then suddenly, he slammed his laptop shut, packed it up and said, "I have to go." He rushed out the door, almost knocking the person coming in over and leaving Andrea sitting there with a frown.

****

"Another therapist, Dr. Calvin Thomas was found this morning. It has only been three days since Dr. O'Neal's murder and this is the fifth victim in the last three weeks. Police are still at the scene gathering evidence. We will continue to keep you posted on this story as it develops."

"Clear!"

Before she could step away from the desk, the director of

the evening news came over to Andrea. "May I speak to you?"

"Sure, Jim," she said before she thanked the sound technician for removing her microphone. Then to Jim, she said, "Would you mind walking with me?" She didn't wait for him to answer; she just began walking.

As they moved through the hall, he said, "I don't think we should cover the serial killer any longer. The numbers show that people aren't interested in the story and all the other networks have stopped covering it."

Andrea stopped, crossed her arms and turned to Jim. "Are you stopping it because I didn't agree with you about covering the dog fighting ring?"

Jim glanced down. "It wasn't my decision to stop covering this story."

Andrea's eyes narrowed; she knew he was lying. She started walking away. Over her shoulder, she said, "Okay, but if we miss out on what happens next, don't say I didn't tell you."

****

"Thank you for coming in during normal office hours. I wanted to apologize in person for the last session. I feel like I can really help you with the abandonment issues and the way that you've coped with them in the past."

"I don't believe you can," Andre said. "You're too focused on *other* parts instead of my mental health."

"No, no, no." Dr. Johnathan Taylor shook his head. "That's not true. I just want to make sure you're healthy, mentally and physically."

Andre stood and the doctor followed.

"You won't report me, will you?" the doctor asked. "I have

a wife and two kids in college. I can't lose my license."

"So that's the real reason you wanted me to come in? I knew you didn't want to help me."

Dr. Taylor missed the slight nod of Andre's head as he walked out of the office.

"But you didn't answer my question."

"And I won't," Andre said over his shoulder.

"You won't what?"

****

The Tennessean

Therapists are still being murdered in the Nashville metropolitan area. For the past month there have been nine victims. The police are baffled as to the motive for the killings and are no closer to finding a suspect.

Here's what we know about the serial killer: The majority of the killings have been near the downtown area. The therapists are all male and were all known to each other. The only thing that the police have ruled out is that the killer is most likely not a woman...

****

"Knock, knock. Can I come in and talk with you?"

Andrea glanced up at Jim. "You're already in. What would you like to talk about?" She put the newspaper down on the coffee table in her dressing room.

Jim tilted his head to take a look at the article she was reading, then, he took the seat across from hers. "You're still keeping up with those murders, I see."

Crossing her arms and legs, she just stared at him. They sat in silence for a few awkward seconds. Before Jim leaned forward, resting his elbows on his knees. "Are you still seeing a therapist?"

"Why?" She frowned at him.

"Well, I see you know another therapist was found two blocks from here and not in his office. So the higher ups want to start covering the killings again." He watched her face closely for any signs of shock. Then he saw the little flicker of interest in her eyes. He glanced down at the article she was just reading and he wondered, *why is she so interested in these murders?*

Even though she was happy to hear this news, she tried to remain neutral. But it was difficult because the mystery of the murders and the serial killer renewed something in her. It made her love being a journalist again instead of just a news reader. "Okay," she finally said. "Are we going to be on location of the murder for this one since this doesn't follow the pattern?"

"No, the police won't allow us at the scene or provide any information beyond what you have there in that article."

Knock! knock!

Both of them turned to her door and when it opened, Andrea jumped up. "Mom, what are you doing here?" Her voice was filled with surprise, but then, she noticed the woman standing next to her mother and she backed up a bit.

Diana Jones stepped into the dressing room and fidgeted with her hands. And then, Andrea noticed the man standing behind her mother and the woman. Andre!

With confusion on her face, Andrea turned back to her mother.

Jim stood. "I'm going to...." He paused, and searched the faces of the two women before he turned to the man. His eyes lingered on Andre's face before he exited from the dressing room.

****

"Baby, I never wanted you to find out what I have to tell you this way," Diana Jones said to her daughter. "Can we sit down?"

Andrea just stared at her mother, still not understanding what was going on. Her mother had introduced the other woman as Deborah Jones and Andrea was trying to answer questions that had not yet been asked.

While Andrea and Andre remained standing, Diane and Deborah sat down. Diane said, "This is my twin sister, Deborah. You've already met your twin brother."

Andrea glanced at him with wide eyes.

"I don't even want to hear this right now." Andrea grabbed her purse before she stomped out of her dressing room. She didn't know where she was going, but she needed to be away from her mother and...the others.

But behind her, she heard his voice. "Hey! Wait! You don't want to hear what they have to tell you?"

Turning to Andre, she said, "Why would I want to do *that* here in my dressing room?"

After a moment, he nodded. "You have a point. So where are you going?"

"I don't know."

"Can I go with you? I want to talk to you."

She didn't say yes or no, she just began walking and Andre followed her. They left the news station walking down James Robertson Parkway toward 5th Avenue N.

They were silent until Andre said, "You know more than you're letting on about what your mom was getting ready to tell you, don't you?"

Andrea just kept walking.

"You figured it out that day in the coffee bar just like I did. The similar names, how much we looked alike. I left you there, I rushed out of that place to get the truth from my mom."

After a moment, Andrea nodded. "You're right, I did. But it was before the coffee bar. I found letters and pictures from your mom when I was fifteen."

His eyes narrowed. "So are you telling me the coffee bar was a setup so we could meet?"

Andrea gave him a shy look glance that was all the answer he needed.

He was not happy. "You are just as bad for your mom. Manipulating bit-"

She turned toward him. "You better not finish that word or *you* will find yourself on the ground."

He laughed. "I doubt that."

Andrea pushed him.

He hardly budged. "It feels good to have a sister to pick a fight with. I wish you'd found me when you found out that I existed."

Andrea walked toward a bench and sat down. She wasn't sure how much she wanted to reveal yet.

When he sat next to her, she said, "I tried, actually. I was seeing a therapist and when I found the letters and pictures, I shared a few with the doctor. I thought I was doing a good thing, but then something crazy happened." She took a deep breath. "The doctor became filled with rage and told me that I was a liar. He snatched the papers from me, then began beating me as if I'd done something to him. I blacked out." She paused and squeezed her eyes shut. "When I regained consciousness, the secretary was calling 911. I later learned Dr. Johnson was your father." She held back a sob. "He did a lot of damage to me. More than before I'd gone to him."

There were long moments of silence before Andre whispered, "Was my father your first kill?"

She gasped and turned to him. "What the? I tell you about a painful experience and you ask was he my first kill? How did you come up with that?"

"I've been following you." He let those words sink in before he continued, "After I went to talk to my mother, we went to talk with your mom. Diane told me that whole story of their decision to separate us at birth. My mom wanted my father so bad that she was willing to do anything to get him. It didn't matter he was married with another child on the way. And since your mother was in love with a married man, too, she was willing to give her sister one of her twins.

"My father exploited my mother. He was her therapist and took advantage of her. And she thought if she had his child, his wife would leave him."

Andrea released a long sigh. "Well that doesn't explain why you think I killed your father."

"Your mother told me."

Andrea pressed her back against the bench.

He continued, "She doesn't know for sure, but one day, you came back from a *walk* wearing different clothing. So, was he your first kill?" he repeated his question.

Andrea closed her eyes and flashed back to the day she was out taking her walk. When she was fifteen....

Why would he treat me like that? He told me he thought of me as his daughter and that I could tell him anything. He lied! The rage, anger and betrayal made her walk faster. He'd sent a message that he was sorry he'd beaten her like he had and that he would no longer be practicing. She already knew that he wouldn't be able to practice because he was being brought up on criminal charges.

She reached his house just as he'd pulled in the driveway. The name plate on the door of his home office showed Dr. Andre Michael Johnson. As he walked into the office, Andrea shoved him with all of her might, knocking him to the floor. He never knew what hit him.

BAM!

"I hate you!"

BAM!

"I trusted you!

Crack!

His body went limp.

****

"In other news, the police have made an arrest in the therapist murders. Former anchorwoman Andrea Jones and her twin brother, Andre Jones were arrested. The police report states that the twins were killing therapists because of the abuse they suffered at the hands of their therapist when they were teens. Andrea made her first kill when she was fifteen after a Dr. Johnson brutally beat her during a therapy session. Andre made his first kill at the same age after his therapist, Dr. John Furth repeatedly raped him. Neither were charged for those murders as they were teens.

"Police still don't know what triggered the recent murders, but they believe there are more murders. More on this story tonight at ten. Stencil Page reporting."

The End

Latasha Holloway *is an avid reader and loves baking in her free time. She's currently working on her first novel. She also hopes to one day open a bakery where other avid readers can come enjoy pastries and read at the same time. Latasha currently resides in Nashville, TN.*

15

MY HUSBAND, HER EX

By Rashonda Jones Aiken

Rage had set up residence in Alexis Martin's home. And she'd opened up the door and invited it in.

"My mother was right about you!" her husband yelled across the bedroom of their apartment.

"What are you talking about, Xavier?" Alexis started to cry, trying to figure out what it was that her set her husband off – this time.

"Shut up your crying and or get out." Xavier was fuming as he paced back and forth across their bedroom. "I can't believe you cheated on me. And with my best friend at that. My mom was right, you just married me for my money." Xavier released a pained laugh. "I thought you were different than the other women I dated."

Alexis's eyes grew wide. Up until this moment, she had no idea why her husband of seven years was going crazy. It had become par for their relationship. He was always mad about something and would just commence to going off on her before getting all the facts. But cheating with his best friend? No wonder he was going ballistic.

"Xavier, I don't know where you got that. I did not cheat on you. I would never do that. I love you! I didn't cheat with anyone, especially not Larry."

"I filed for divorce, Lexi," he said, his tone dry like he was done talking.

Alexis was dumbfounded. She knew her marriage wasn't always rosy, but she never thought it would come to an end like this. She wanted to fight some more, explain to her husband how mistaken he was. But she was tired. Today, it was Larry. Last month, it was the barista at Starbucks. It was always something. Always *somebody*. And she was tired of trying to save a marriage that didn't seem like it could be saved. She just sighed in defeat and retreated to the sofa in hopes that Xavier's rant would pass – like it did every other time.

"Fine, Xavier," she said. "Just know that you're wrong. I love you and want to spend the rest of my life with you."

***

It had been two weeks since Alexis had talked to her husband. They walked around the house as estranged roommates. She'd tried a couple of times to engage him, but Xavier wasn't having it. That's why when she received his text to come home asap, she dropped everything and came running.

"Xavier?" she called out as soon as she stepped through

the door. "I'm here."

Her heart raced as she waited, hoping for him to rush into her arms and apologize for being such a jerk. Their makeup sex was always the bomb and she felt a flutter in her stomach when she thought about it.

"I'm in the den," he called out.

The smile left her face as soon as she stepped into the den and saw him sitting on the sofa, a cigar smoldering in the tray, an almost-empty glass of Bourbon on the table next to it. He was eerily relaxed and the flutter in Alexis' stomach turned into a typhoon.

"What's going on?" Alexis asked.

Xavier didn't say a word as he stood, walked over to her and handed her some papers.

"Those are divorce papers. I'm hoping you'll sign and end this fiasco of a marriage."

Alexis stood trembling, a mixture of disbelief and fury running through her body as she examined the papers. *How long had he been planning this?*

Before she could say a word, he said, "I had the maid pack your bags."

Alexis swallowed, fought back her tears and said, "So, just like that we're over?"

He turned his back. "You should've thought about that before you screwed my friend."

They stood in silence, until she turned and left the room. Was her marriage really ending on a lie? Part of her wanted to plead, beg him to not throw them away, but she knew her husband. Nothing she could say would change his mind.

Alexis stuffed the papers in her purse, grabbed her bags and left out the front door. She turned and took one last look, pushing back the bile in her throat. This had been her home for seven years. They'd never been blessed with children, but she was still hopeful. Or she *used* to be hopeful.

She loaded up her stuff in the back of her gray Lexus RX SUV. As soon as she pulled out of the long driveway and onto the street, the sadness overtook her. She sobbed so hard she had to pull over at the corner. Her heart was just broken into a thousand pieces.

After about twenty minutes, Alexis tried to pull herself together and contemplated her next move.

She took a deep breath, then called her sister, Andrea, to tell her the news. The phone rang, then went to voicemail. Andrea had been MIA for the past two weeks and Alexis desperately needed her sister. She hung up crying and kept driving.

Alexis headed to The Four Seasons Hotel. She parked and went inside to get a room for a couple of nights until she figured out her next step.

A tall thin woman with brunette hair greeted her at the front desk.

"Hello, my name is Melanie, how can I assist you today?"

"Hi, I'd like a suite for three nights." She pulled out her American Express credit card.

The woman smiled as she took it, then swiped the card. After a few seconds, the woman said, "Sorry, madam, your card has declined."

Alexis frowned. "Please try it again."

Melanie swiped it again, and it declined again. "Sorry madam, but do you have another card?" She had the nerve to still be smiling.

Tears streamed down her face as she tried to figure out

what to do. She couldn't believe that Xavier cancelled her credit card. She wiped her tears and said, "I'll be right back."

Alexis went out to her SUV to get her tote bag. She kept an emergency secured credit card in her glove compartment – a piece of advice her mother had given her before her death. At the time, Alexis thought her mom was doing the most. Now, she was grateful.

Fifteen minutes later, Alexis was settled in her room, trying to figure out her next move. Her sister was a lawyer – one of the best in town. She'd know what Alexis should do. Alexis called Andrea again, to no avail.

"Sis, I need you," Alexis said once her sister's automated voicemail message had finished playing. "Please call me back. Or better yet, come to the Four Seasons on Raritan Road, room 612. You're not going to believe what happened."

Alexis hung the phone up, then laid across the bed and cried herself to sleep.

****

Andrea saw her sister's phone call, but Alexis always came with drama and after the day she'd had at work – one of her cases had been tossed out – the last thing she felt like doing was faking it with her baby sister. Especially after the text she'd just received.

It's done.

Those words should've made her feel better. After all, it's what she'd been praying for the past seven years. Instead, Andrea felt sick to her stomach. It wasn't done until her sister knew the truth.

****

I'm really getting a divorce.

The reality woke Alexis out of her sleep. This wasn't like all the other times when Xavier came out of whatever madness he was in. Alexis knew that in her gut. This time, it was for real.

"I have to talk to Andrea," Alexis muttered as she threw back the covers and stood up. She was still in her clothes from last night so she removed them and jumped in the shower.

Her stomach reminded her to grab a bagel from the coffee shop on her way through the hotel lobby. Alexis really didn't want to stop because she was trying to catch Andrea at the daycare center, where she always dropped Adam, her son, off before heading to work.

Andrea was one of those people who never deviated from her routine, so Alexis was sure she'd catch her sister if she made it there by 8. Something was obviously wrong with her sister's phone and this was the only way she could catch up with Andrea to tell her about Xavier.

Alexis cursed at the traffic, but made it to the daycare center at 8:03. She said a silent prayer that she hadn't missed her sister, and pulled up just as Andrea and Adam were getting out the car.

"Auntie Lexi!" Adam exclaimed when he saw her. He raced over to hug her. "I haven't seen you in forever. What are you doing here?"

Alexis relished her nephew's embrace. "I missed you," she said. "Just wanted to see you before you went to school."

He flashed a toothy grin. "Well, now you see me!"

"Yep, and my day is complete." She looked up at Andrea. "I've been calling you. What's going on with your phone?"

She shifted, a nervous expression crossed her face.

"Oh, ah, my phone…it's not working."

"Mommy, you were just on your phone," Adam said.

"That was my work phone, Sweetie," Andrea said. "Well, let me get him inside. We're already late."

"I need to talk to you," Alexis said, not missing her sister's reaction. Something was off.

Andrea shifted again. "Ummm, well-"

"I'll wait out here for you to go drop Adam off."

Andrea looked like she wanted to protest, but simply said, "Okay."

As she walked away, Alexis had a strange feeling in her gut. Had Xavier already told Andrea about the divorce? Nah. The two of them never got along. They could barely stand to be in the same room, so it wasn't that.

It seemed like an eternity before Andrea returned to her car and if Alexis didn't know better, she'd swear her sister was avoiding her.

Finally, Andrea emerged from the building. Her eyes were red like she'd been crying.

"What's up, Lexi," Andrea said as she approached her sister.

"I was trying to catch up with you to tell you Xavier filed for divorce."

The expression on her sister's face told her this news wasn't new.

"Good."

"What do you mean, good? I know you don't like him, but this is my husband we're talking about. He accused me of cheating with his best friend and filed for divorce!"

Andrea's shoulders slumped. "He's always accusing you of cheating, Lexi. He's a jerk and you're better off without him. You settled for that dysfunctional relationship for years as it is."

Alexis didn't know if it was because her emotions were high or what, but she snapped.

"I don't believe you. I'm devastated about my marriage ending and not only do you not answer my multiple calls but then you're so callous about it all!" Alexis cried. "You never have supported my marriage. You may have this high-powered job and a kid you don't even have time for, but you're empty inside and you want everyone to be as miserable as you!"

Andrea's eyes bucked. "Wow. Just wow." She held up her hands. "I understand you're upset, so I'm gonna let you make it-"

"No," Alexis said, cutting her off. "Since mom died we're all each other has and you've been jealous of me, especially my marriage to Xavier."

Andrea busted out laughing, then gritted her teeth as she took a step toward Alexis. "Nobody's jealous of you or your no-good man."

"At least I got a man."

"Had. You had a man."

"I don't know why I thought I could come to you. Ever since I got married, you've been hating."

Andrea took slow deep breaths, like she was trying to weigh her next words. Finally, she said, "Sissy, I've never been jealous of your man. Because he used to be mine."

"What?"

Andrea sighed and took a step back. "Look, Lexi. I never wanted this to come out like this. And I've let you parade around her like you'd snagged some grand prize for years, but I dated Red in college."

"I remember you dating Red. What does that have to do with anything?"

"Red is Xavier. It's what his fraternity brothers called him."

Alexis stared at her sister in shock.

"W-what?"

"I broke up with him because he's a jealous, crazed, cheating dog."

"H-how could you not t-tell me?"

"Because by the time I met the dude, you were freaking married, remember? I was away at law school and came home to you announcing that y'all were married. Then, mama died and the timing never seemed right. You were too far in love."

Alexis paced back and forth in front of her sister's car. She wanted to call her sister a lie, but memories that flashed through her mind, told her it was the truth.

How they always seemed to be angry whispering.

How Andrea despised Xavier.

How Xavier despised Andrea.

"D-did Xavier know?" Alexis finally asked.

"Not only did he know, he targeted you to get back at me. That's why I can't stand him."

Alexis was about to say something else, when a hard reality dawned on her. "W-wait. Isn't Red Adam's father?"

Andrea's non-answer was her answer.

Alexis collapsed against the car in tears.

Andrea went to hug her sobbing sister. "I'm sorry I didn't

tell you. You were just so happy and you needed that after Mama's death. But I promise you, I'm going to make this up to you. And we're going to take Xavier for every penny he's worth."

The End

Rashonda Jones Aiken *is an avid reader and an aspiring author who has the love of writing many anthologies. Check out her website www.rahwaygirlzpublishing.com.*

Check out these other

anthologies from

Brown Girls Books…

www.BrownGirlsBooks.com